AMISH MERCY

THE AMISH BONNET SISTERS BOOK 1

SAMANTHA PRICE

CHAPTER 1

Florence Baker released her foot from the pedal of her sewing machine and looked out the window with longing. Today, her fresh-air wander through the apple trees would have to wait.

"Florence! Why are you staring out the window?" Mercy looked over her shoulder. "My dress is nowhere near done. Can't you sew faster?"

Mercy's voice grated on Florence's nerves. She turned away from the half-made dress and glared at Mercy. *"Nee.* Leave me be. *Dat* always said children shouldn't see things half done."

"I'm not a child. I'm eighteen." Mercy put her hands on her hips.

"Numbers don't always tell the story. You act like a child." Florence turned back to her machine. "I don't know why *Mamm* thinks you're mature enough to marry."

"I am mature. You're only being mean to me because *Mamm's* in the kitchen and can't hear you."

Florence huffed and looked back at Mercy. "If *Gott* wants you to marry, the man will appear from wherever he is and find you. He'll bring the two of you together somehow."

"He won't have to because *Mamm's* helping me." A smirk hinted around Mercy's perfect bow-shaped lips. She always had an answer for everything.

"I don't like all this deception sur-rounding this man coming to dinner. I'd say he doesn't know people have conspired against him."

"The Bergers said their nephew could help with the harvest this season and they would've told him about me too, I'm sure." Mercy poked out her tongue. "So there."

Florence shook her head in complete disgust and knew this nonsense wouldn't be happening if their father were alive. "You expect to fall in love and live happily ever after and never have any problems because your love will be sufficient? Is that right?"

"Jah." Mercy laughed. "You'll see. I'll be happy and have three *bopplis* before you even think about getting married. Oh, wait. You'll still be here at home with *Mamm,* doing the same old thing."

"Someone has to keep everything running." Florence turned back to her machine and put her foot down, hoping the hum would put a stop to Mercy's talking or drown out her whining. Florence wasn't sure how it had all come about that Ada Berger was convinced her sister's son was the perfect man for Mercy. All she knew was that *Mamm* and Ada had gotten their heads together and now Mercy believed Ada's nephew was her husband-to-be.

Mercy had moved right next to her and when Florence caught sight of her out of the corner of her eye, she jumped. Her sister looked annoyed. "What?" asked Florence, thoroughly exasperated.

"I'm goin' to marry Stephen Wilkes and I don't care what you say."

"You can't say that for certain. What if you don't like him when you meet him?"

"I'm still going to marry him just to get away from here." She lowered her head and moved closer to Florence. "And to get away from you."

Florence gasped, more than a little hurt by the comment. "Why would you say that? Haven't I looked after you well enough? I've done the best I could to make you and your sisters happy."

"That was my job as the eldest, but I've never been able to be the eldest because of you." Mercy planted her fists on her hips. "I want to be in charge of something and when I'm married, I'll be boss of my own *haus.*" She stomped away.

Since nobody was around, Florence allowed her tears to flow. Nothing had been the same since her father had died. Her stepmother was good to her, kind and loving, but still there was a gaping hole in her heart.

Mercy wasn't grateful for all Florence had given up for the family. She could've gone to the young people's events looking for a husband. Instead, she'd worked hard in the orchard while delaying any plans of having a family of her own.

Mamm came hurrying out of the kitchen with a dust rag in her hands. "Were you two squabbling?"

"Not really." Florence wiped her eyes and moved the fabric slightly so it would sit tighter under the needle.

"You're upset."

"I'm okay." Florence didn't want to bother her stepmother with anything that would worry her, so she did what she always did when she was upset; she kept working.

When *Mamm* was dusting the mantle over the fireplace, Mercy came back into the room. "My dress should be finished by now, *Mamm*. I want it perfect for tomorrow night and she's not finished it."

"If Florence says it'll be done, then it'll be done," *Mamm* said.

"*Jah,* but I want it done today and not tomorrow. What if I want to make some changes? She always makes them too long."

"That's easily solved." Florence swung around to face her. "You can do the hem once I've finished."

"Be grateful she's sewing your dress at

all, Mercy," *Mamm* said. "It's a special treat and I've taken money out of our savings for it."

"*Denke, Mamm*. I do appreciate it, I do, but she's always sewing and won't let me have a go."

Florence had taught all her sisters to sew, but she ignored that comment not wanting to get into an argument. "It will be ready." Florence didn't even look up when she added, "Now go away and leave me to concentrate!"

"Humph. Rude!" Mercy said. "Did you hear how she spoke to me, *Mamm?*"

Mamm had moved on to dusting the wide wooden arm rests of the couch. She always went into a cleaning frenzy when they were having special guests for dinner. There was one guest in particular she was hoping to impress, on behalf of Mercy.

"*Mamm,* will you answer me?" Mercy asked.

Mamm reacted to the frequent arguments of her daughters by ignoring them completely. It was often up to Florence to step in, but this time Florence was involved. While Florence turned her attention to the sewing, *Mamm* finally spoke. "She's the best seamstress out of the lot of you. Do you want to look pretty tomorrow night or not?"

Mercy pouted. "I do but … Hey, wait. Did you just say I'm not as good at sewing as Florence?"

When *Mamm* hesitated, Florence said, "I'm better only because I've been doing it longer."

"Only because you're always on the sewing machine and I don't get a chance."

"Keep cleaning, Mercy. Do you want Stephen to think we have a dirty *haus?* He'll think you'll make a dreadful *fraa.*"

"It's fine. It's good enough already."

"Help me clean. Get a rag from the kitchen."

When Mercy was out of the room, Florence stopped the machine. "Does Stephen even want to get married, *Mamm?*"

"He would. Why wouldn't he? I also know he hasn't got a girlfriend. Ada told me so much about him. He's her older *shweschder's* middle son. She has three and none of them is married."

"Why aren't they trying to marry off the oldest one?" Right now, Florence wasn't the least bit concerned about Ada's nephews. What she'd asked was meant as a big hint to *Mamm,* since *Mamm* wasn't the least concerned about finding a husband for her. It also made it worse because she, not Mercy, was the eldest of the girls.

"She didn't say why. She recommended Stephen instead. I guess she likes him better."

Florence frowned, not liking the hurtful implications of that answer. *Mamm* kept dusting, unaware of what she'd just said and how it related to Florence and Mercy. Adding to Florence's upset was the fact that the conversations she'd overheard between Wilma and Ada were all about finding a nice man for Mercy, whom *Mamm* had referred to as 'my eldest.'

At first, Florence had tried not to think about it, but it had festered in her mind like a forgotten piece of bread left in the back of a cupboard. She'd always thought of Wilma as her mother and had called her *Mamm* since she was four. Didn't Wilma see her as one of her daughters? Florence turned away from the machine and said, "So is the older *bruder* a stepson?"

There was no chance for her stepmother to even hear her question, much less to answer it, because loud screams rang from outside. It was Florence's two youngest half-sisters hollering at the top of their lungs. "Florence! Florence, the Graingers' cows are out again!" she heard Cherish yelling.

"*Ach nee!* Not again. Florence, will you see about that?" *Mamm* asked.

Florence was always the one sent to talk with people, whether it was the Graingers from next door or people who came to the door of their home. The cows had gotten out just weeks ago, and Doug Grainger had promised to fix the fence and make it stronger.

Florence bounded to her feet. "Okay." She left the dress draped over the sewing table and headed out of the house. She was glad her stepmother hadn't heard that last question. She'd regretted the words as quickly as they'd flown off her tongue. Of course, *Mamm* preferred her own children to her stepdaughter, but she shouldn't make it so obvious.

When Florence stepped outside onto the porch, she was faced with her two youngest half-sisters. Each carried a bucket of windfall apples. It was one of their chores to pick up the apples that fell before the harvest.

Florence walked closer and looked in the buckets to see they hadn't gathered many. They had hundreds of apple trees and picking up those apples from the floor of the orchard was an important job. "Is that all you got?"

Favor held up the bucket as she shook her head. "There are more."

"We haven't finished yet," Cherish added.

"Sort those and then get the rest while I talk to Mr. Grainger," she told the girls.

The apples they'd collected were to be divided into three groups—eating apples, apples suitable for cooking or making into cider, and apples that were good for nothing but to be thrown into the compost heap.

"Can I come too?" Cherish, the youngest called out. "I want to hear what you say to him."

Florence turned around. *"Nee.* You do your chores and then see what *Mamm* wants you to do in the *haus.* We've guests coming tomorrow for dinner." They all knew that meant everything had to be spotless.

"We wanna come too," Favor said in a whine much like Mercy's.

"*Nee*. Stay here." Florence glared at them, almost daring them to defy her. She had to be stern with all the girls or they'd do whatever they liked. They'd already stopped listening to *Mamm* because she wasn't firm enough.

When Florence was a distance from the house, she heard Favor call out, "Say hello to old Mr. Grainger." Then she heard Cherish giggling along with Favor. Mr. Grainger was gruff and they knew Florence didn't like speaking with him.

She yelled back, "Just get the rest of those windfalls picked up. On my way back, I'm going to check you've gotten them all." Florence kept walking. Each day she tried to get away and be alone amongst the trees. It was where she felt close to her father. He'd loved his apple trees and perhaps that was why she loved being amongst them. Out here in the fresh air, the breeze blew her troubles away, and the trees smelled like happiness and comfort.

She stopped and touched a ripe red Fuji apple, and memories of her father introducing that variety to the orchard jumped into her mind. He'd told her it was a variety developed in Japan—a cross between the Red Delicious and the Ralls Janet apples. They had a reputation for being good for both eating and baking, along with the added bonus that they stored well.

There was another reason Florence felt good in the orchard. She was surrounded by history. Not only the history of her own family, but the early American settlers who had grown their apples from seeds after traveling from their home countries. Her father's passion had been collecting those early varieties, the ones that still had the same properties and lineage as those from the early days. They were dying out as the more popular hybrid varieties took over. When she got some spare time, she intended to search out some of those rare varieties herself.

With her fingers still wrapped around the Fuji apple, she twisted it off the branch. She held it in the air and admired how perfect it was with the tiny stem still attached.

Her mouth watered. It'd been ages since breakfast and there was nothing like a fresh apple plucked from the tree. She polished it on her apron and then sank her teeth into it as she started walking again. The Graingers didn't have too many cows, and hopefully Doug Grainger had heard the girls screaming and was already moving the cows back to his own property.

Still worried about her sister rushing into marriage, she dragged her feet. There was nothing she could do. *Mamm* approved of it and Mercy had her mind made up. What upset her most was she herself was twenty-four, a good six years older than Mercy. Did her stepmother hope to keep her around to run the place? Is that why *Mamm* wasn't bothering to find her a husband? Actually, she could think of nothing worse than being set up. Love would happen if it was meant to be. That was what she'd told Mercy, and that was what she believed.

Once she'd finished the apple, she placed the core at the base of a tree so she could collect it on her way home.

When she came to the border of the two properties, she walked past three cows happily eating the fallen Red Delicious apples. As she got closer to the Grainger's house, her foot caught on a rock and it caused her to trip. Instinctively, her hands flew up in front to save her face from smacking into the dirt. The day was getting worse by the second.

She picked herself up, looked at her grazed and stinging palms, and then dusted the dirt from her white apron with her fingertips. It was then she noticed her *kapp* on the ground. Embarrassed, and afraid someone might see her without it, she snatched it up and popped it back on her head. As she tied the long strings under her chin to prevent it coming off again, she noticed someone walking toward her. Someone far too handsome to be Mr. Grainger.

CHAPTER 2

"HELLO," the man called out. He was tall. His slim fitting jeans, loose white button-up shirt, and short-cropped dark hair let her know that, just like the Graingers, he was an *Englischer*.

She fixed a smile on her face and wondered if he was minding the house while the Graingers were away. "Hello," she replied when he got a little closer. "I'm looking for Doug Grainger."

She stared up into his dark hazel eyes, admiring how they were fringed with long dark lashes. Suddenly she was nervous because this man was a dream-come-true even with his two-days' growth of beard.

He thoughtfully shook his finger at her, and then briefly pointed at her. "You're one of the bonnet sisters."

She stared at him, wondering what he was talking about. "No."

"You've got the most incredible blue eyes."

She did her best to hide the pleasure she felt from his compliment. She got so few of those ... Especially with her attractive half-sisters always close by.

When she didn't speak, he asked, "Are they real?"

It was an odd thing to ask but the absence of a smile told her he wasn't joking. She tilted her head. "Whatever do you mean?"

"Are they colored contact lenses?"

"Oh. No. They're my very own eyes."

"They're beautiful." He stood staring at her and smiling.

"Um, 'bonnet sisters,' you said?"

"I see you all going past in your buggies and you've all got those white bonnets, and you're all sisters. The Graingers told me a little about you girls. I've found myself calling you the bonnet sisters—just talking to myself, that's all." He looked pleased for a reason Florence couldn't understand especially since he freely admitted talking to himself.

Suddenly, he lost all appeal and she was jolted back to the reason she was here—the cows! "Where are the Graingers?"

"They've gone. Moved away. They sold this place to me."

"Oh. That's a surprise. Then these are your cows?" She glanced over at the intruders happily munching on her family's income.

"I guess so."

She sighed. If he was their new neighbor, she wasn't going to stand for the 'bonnet sisters' nonsense. Putting aside the issue of the cows that suddenly didn't seem as important as checking him on his rudeness, she touched her *kapp* with her fingertips. "These are prayer *kapps.*"

"*Kapps,* bonnets ... they're all the same to me."

Now she knew he was just an ignorant man, and he might as well stay that way. "I'm here about the cows, not our head-coverings."

"Do you want to buy them? I'll sell them to you. The Graingers left them with the farm."

"'Buy them?'" Now she knew they weren't going to get along with this man any better than they had with the former neighbors.

He nodded. "I'll take a reasonable sum. I don't want to rob anyone."

"Oh, well, that's good to know. But why would I buy them? They're eating my apples."

"So that's a no?"

"Yes that's a no. Can you get them away from the apples before they devour them all? We use the dropped ones too, and soon your cows will start pulling the lower-hanging fruit from the trees." She wasn't normally unfriendly, but the upset with Mercy and then the fall had caused her to lose patience. Now to find the Graingers had sold, without even offering to sell the land back to them, had further upset her. She gently rubbed her sore palms. "Can you move the cows please?" She noticed an expensive-looking white SUV parked close to the house. Surely the man understood economics. "We need to sell the apples because they're our livelihood. Unless you'd like to buy this year's produce to feed your cows?"

He frowned and rubbed his stubbly

square chin. "I don't think so. That sounds costly."

"Then fix the fence. Or I'll have to charge you for what they've eaten."

"I can fix it."

Looking him up and down, she sincerely doubted he could fix a fence or had ever done any kind of manual labor. "Thanks," she said in reference to him saying he'd fix the fence.

"I'll do my best with the fence. Something like that shouldn't be too hard."

"My father had an agreement with Doug before he sold him the place that Doug would always keep the fence in good order." Had her father known the Graingers' would bring bothersome cows to their property, he might've thought twice about selling them the parcel of land. At the time, though, they'd needed the money—they'd had three poor-producing seasons in a row. It was a rough patch and it came in the years directly following her father's marriage to Wilma.

There were more mouths to feed and at that time Florence's two older brothers were too young to find work to help out the family.

"Your father owned the place before Doug?"

"That's right. Didn't Doug tell you about the importance of maintaining the fences?"

"No, but I will do everything I can to keep the horses out of the orchard."

"They're cows."

"I meant cows." He chuckled and then scratched his head. "I'm just not sure how to get the cows back here. How would I get them to do what I say?"

"You herd them. They're cows."

"I'm well aware they're cows. Even though I accidentally said 'horses' a minute ago. I know that much."

Florence sighed. It was either offer to help, or go back and finish sewing the horri- bly-ungrateful Mercy's dress while listening to her nag and whine. Either choice was as unappealing as the other. If she helped the new neighbor, at least she'd be out in the fresh air for longer. "Would you like me to help?"

A smile spread over his face. "I'd appreciate it. I have no idea what to do."

She looked him up and down once more. "Neither do I really, but I probably have a better idea than you. I just hope my hands hold out." She looked at her palms that were now red. The skin hadn't broken so she was pleased about that.

"You've hurt yourself?" He put out his hands for her to show him, but she pulled her hands back against herself.

"They'll be okay. Let's get this done, shall we? I've got lots of other things I need to do today."

Together they pulled back the fallen down fence so the cows would have a wider area to move through. Then Florence had a brainstorm. "Do you have hay?"

"Plenty of it stored up for the winter. And it'll be winter soon."

She nodded. "Bring some and put it on your side of the fence."

"Hmm, hay or apples. Which would they prefer?"

"Hopefully the hay. You get all the hay you can carry and then I'll try to move them away from the apples and herd them back through the fence. Once they're through and onto your land, we can fix the fence."

"Okay."

CHAPTER 3

IT ONLY TOOK fifteen minutes to get the cows back on his side of the fence. When the cows paid little attention to the hay, Florence had lured them back to their own property with handfuls of apples.

When they had pulled the broken fence mostly closed, he said, "Thanks, I couldn't have done this without you."

She stood close to the small gap in the fence, on his side, knowing that everyone back home would be wondering what had taken her so long. Mercy would be annoyed she wasn't finishing off the dress, but all of that seemed so far away as the sun danced on her skin while a cool breeze tickled her face.

He picked up one of the apples from the ground and then straightened up while he stared at it. "Delicious, right?"

"Yes, that's right. They're a variety that's less popular than it was once. The Fuji and the Honeycrisps have taken over–at least for us. The Granny Smiths have always stayed a firm favorite."

He chuckled. "Sounds like a sales pitch."

"It's not. And we need to truly fix the fence, now."

"I saw wire in the barn."

"Fetch it, and pliers."

WITH THE NEIGHBOR'S pliers and some wire he'd found in his barn, Florence fixed the fence the best she could with her sore hands.

Looking at her handiwork, she said, "It'll do for the moment, but since they've tasted my apples, I know they'll try it again. The fence needs to be strengthened all along this side, and as I said before—"

"I know. Your father sold it to the previous owner with the understanding he'd look after the fence. Even though my contract had nothing of the kind on it, I'll honor that original agreement. I'll trust you're not making up stories."

"I'm not. Trust me." She smiled. "Anyway, thank you. Before you interrupted me, though, I was going to say you could run barbed wire across the top or electric tape. Both things work well, I'm told."

"I'll look into them."

His gaze traveled to her mid-section.

She looked down to see her soiled dress and apron. "Look at my clothes."

He grimaced. "I'm trying not to."

"They're ruined." It was incredible that his white shirt had remained crisp and clean, despite having carried hay and fencing wire.

"I'm sorry. Let me pay for it."

"It's not the money. It's the time it takes to sew." She cleared her throat, shocked at how much her whining tone reminded her of one of her younger sisters. "Thanks anyway. It's an old dress and I'm sure the stains will come out adequately with a good soak. I'm surprised Doug didn't tell you about the fence agreement." She frowned at him. "Are you a city man?"

"How can you tell?"

"Believe me it wasn't difficult."

He looked over at the apple trees. "They do look tasty. No wonder the cows want to eat them."

"We start picking on Monday, officially." She thought she'd be neighborly. It was the right thing to do. "I can bring you some. We grow a few different varieties. One for everyone's tastes."

"No, that's okay."

"I will. I'll bring you a bucketful. Some are good for eating and we've got others better for cooking. The Granny Smiths are wonderful in pies and you can do all kinds of other cooking with them. We sell our apple goods, too, and cider in our shop at the front of our house near the road."

"I've seen the shop. When do you open that?"

"Monday. I'm cleaning it tomorrow so it's ready for opening day."

"I wouldn't mind half a dozen apples. Eating ones. I don't do that sort of cooking. And I'll strengthen that fence even more tomorrow. Is it a deal?" He put his hand out, above the fence, and she showed him her grazed palms and he put his hand back down by his side.

"It's a deal," she said.

He held her gaze and she stared across the fence into his dark hazel eyes. Her former attraction was sparked once more. It was a shame he didn't know what he was doing on a farm. Uselessness was such an unattractive trait in a man. It was an even greater shame he was an off limits *Englisher*.

"Goodbye, Mr. …"

"I'm Carter."

"Hello, Mr. Carter. I'm Florence Baker."

He laughed. "I'm sorry. Forgive me for laughing. Carter's my first name. I'm Carter Braithwaite. I didn't think folks would be so formal around here." He placed his hands casually on his hips. "We are neighbors after all. Seems you called the previous owner by his first name."

"We hardly spoke to him because he kept his cows in. Well, most of the time he did. They got out a few weeks ago."

He smiled at her and for a second, she wondered if he was attracted to her, and then he ruined the moment by saying, "I'm pleased to meet one of the bonnet sisters at last."

She grimaced. Even though he was handsome, he was offensive. Just when she was contemplating telling him so, he spoke again.

"How many sisters do you have?"

"Six. Plus me. I'm the eldest."

"I see. I thought you might be."

"And why's that?" Did she look so old? Everyone always thought she was much older than she was.

"You've got an air of authority about you. Like you're running the show."

"Hmm." She didn't know how to take that. "I've got two older brothers. Technically, I'm not the eldest, but I'm the eldest living at home. Also, the eldest girl." She was the youngest child of her late mother, but she didn't need to tell him too much.

"Why didn't your father come to tell me about the cows?"

"That would be a challenge. He died a couple of years ago."

"Oh," he said with raised eyebrows. "I'm sorry to hear that."

"My older brothers have left home. One got married and lives quite close but the other moved to Ohio soon after our father died."

"You're running an orchard and there are no men at home?"

"Yes. We're fine. We have seasonal workers who help."

He tipped his head to one side. "Who's managing the place?"

"Me and my mother, mostly. My stepmother."

"And your mother?"

"She died when I was quite small." She hadn't wanted to tell him all that since they'd only just met. "And what about you?"

"Me?" he asked.

"Do you have family? It's your turn to tell me. It's only fair."

He chuckled. "Are you trying to find out if I'm married?"

She inhaled deeply. "No. I didn't even think ..."

"Oh. I'm so unappealing you thought no one would marry me?" He looked down at the ground.

"Are you ... married?" she asked.

He looked back at her and smiled. "No."

"That's what I thought."

He laughed. "Why's that?"

"For one thing, I don't see a woman around."

"Hmm. Did you ever stop to think she might be out working to help support me and these cows?"

Florence couldn't help but giggle. "I wouldn't believe that. You'd be the one working if you were married, wouldn't you? Your wife would stay at home, or she could work too, but she wouldn't work while you just laze about the place."

He laughed again. "I'm not lazing about. I was busy with something before you interrupted me this morning and, just so you know, it's just me alone in the world."

"Sometimes being alone is a good thing."

"Spoken like someone who's never *had* to be alone."

They smiled at one another, until she said, "I better get back to—"

"Back to your bonnet sisters?"

She opened her mouth in shock. Didn't he know how derogatory that sounded? "Please don't call us that."

He grinned and instantly became disturbingly more handsome. "And I have to get back to my chess game."

She scrunched her brows and glanced over at his house. "I thought you lived alone."

"I do."

"Doesn't it take two people to play chess?"

"Not when you have a computer."

"Ah, you play against the computer? That is your opponent?"

"That's right."

"Wouldn't it win every time?"

He chuckled. "I could be a chess genius for all you know. Actually, it has different skill levels. I'm not that good, but I'm learning."

It seemed like a complete waste of one's time. "Goodbye," she uttered before she turned and hurried away.

The brief exchange with the *Englisher* had made her feel lighter inside, which surprised her considering how different he was from any man she'd met before.

CHAPTER 4

MERCY WANTED to give herself the best chance of marrying the man coming to dinner tomorrow night. A brand-new dress might've seemed a small thing, but she desperately wanted to make a good first impression and every detail had to be perfect. That included her appearance. Many people had told her she was attractive with her reddish-brown hair and greenish-blue eyes, but she wouldn't be that attractive in an old black hand-me-down dress. That was why she'd talked *Mamm* into allowing her to have a new one.

For years, she'd dreamed of having her own home and raising her own *kinner*. Apart from getting out from under the shadow Florence cast, she'd be the one to make all the decisions and look after everything and everyone. Best of all, she wouldn't have Florence telling her what to do all day every day. Florence had always been better at everything—in fact, she was more like a second mother than an older sister.

While her younger sisters were busy in the kitchen making the midday meal, Mercy picked up the half-finished dress that Florence had left near the sewing machine. "*Mamm,* she hasn't even finished it. It's taking so long." Her mother was sitting on the couch and had been just about to put her teacup to her lips.

She lowered her cup back to the saucer and placed it on the coffee table in front of her. "There's other things she's had on her mind. Anyway, you don't need it to be finished until tomorrow evening. Have some patience for once in your life. She's making it out of the kindness of her heart."

"I wanted to do it. I want to make sure it's perfect." What she really wanted was to sit down and finish it herself, but she knew Florence was a *wunderbaar* seamstress. That was, when Florence put her mind to it and wasn't distracted with other things.

Mamm continued, "Florence has always done a good job with dresses for you girls."

Mercy sighed. "I know. Where is she anyway? Hasn't she been gone for an awfully long time?"

"Why don't you go look for her if you're worried?" Wilma picked up her cup once more and settled back into the couch and sipped her hot tea.

Mercy spun on her heel. "I will." She walked out the door, jumped down the three front porch steps in one go, and when she looked up she saw Florence walking back to the house. "About time," she mumbled under her breath. Then she hurried to meet her to find out what had taken so long. When she got closer, she saw Florence's clothes were filthy. "What happened to you?"

Florence rolled her eyes. "We have a new neighbor. He didn't know how to get the cows back, so I had to help him. He had no idea about fencing, either, so I had to make a temporary fence repair too."

"That's awful."

She glanced down at her clothes. "I fell in the dirt as well."

"Mr. and Mrs. Grainger aren't there anymore?"

"*Nee.*"

"That's weird."

"I know. I would've expected them to tell us they were going, or at least say goodbye. The new neighbor's interesting."

"In what way?"

"He's an *Englischer* and he's living there by himself. He knows nothing about cows—and from the looks of him, nothing about much else."

Mercy put her hand over her mouth and giggled. "He can't be as cranky as old Mr. Grainger. Anyway, are you going to keep working on my dress?"

"Of course. I'll clean up and have something to eat and then I'll finish it. I know it doesn't look it, but it's nearly done. You can do the hem, can't you?"

"I can."

"Good."

Mercy knew there was something different about Florence. She didn't seem quite so disagreeable. Did it have something to do with the *Englischer?* "Was he handsome?"

Florence glanced over at her as the pair walked side-by-side. "Who?"

"The new neighbor."

"He was a bit rude. Well, not so much rude, he was ... *different.*"

"Keep away from *Englischers*. He's handsome and you liked him. I can tell. Don't tell Joy you like him or she'll give you a lecture about—"

"He is handsome, but I've no interest in him as a man. I would never get involved with an *Englischer.*"

"Is he living there by himself? Just him and the cows?"

"Enough about him. I can't wait for us all to meet Stephen tomorrow night."

Mercy was happy to talk about her husband-to-be.

DURING THE MIDDAY MEAL, the conversation between *Mamm* and the girls was all about Stephen and Mercy's upcoming marriage. Florence was horrified and had to say something to stop the nonsense. If only *Dat* was around to caution Mercy on falling in love with a man she'd never spoken with, or even so much as exchanged letters with.

"Just be careful, Mercy. You need to choose a husband wisely." Florence's best friend had married in haste some years ago and she'd confided in Florence that she regretted it daily.

"I'm sure he's the one. If he doesn't suit me I can change him into the man I want him to be."

"I don't think it works like that." Florence shook her head and wished she could give Liza's unhappiness as a real-life example, but her friend had sworn her to secrecy.

"Oh, coming from someone who hasn't even had a boyfriend. Have you ever even liked anyone?" Joy asked, snatching up the last piece of bread that Florence was reaching for.

With all the bread gone, Florence picked

up the dish of boiled potatoes and spooned two onto her plate. *"Nee,* but it's common sense. You don't want to end up living apart from your husband."

"Like Ira and Mary Schwartz?" Joy asked.

"Jah, like them." They were another example besides Florence's friend.

Joy said, "Everyone knows they just don't get along anymore."

"Not every marriage within the faith is going to work as well as you might think. You can't rush into it and you can't marry just anyone. You've got to have things in common and … and all that."

"We'll have *Gott* and our beliefs in common, and if he looks okay I'm going to marry him." When Florence heaved a sigh, Mercy patted Florence's shoulder. "It'll be okay. I've prayed about it. I asked *Gott* to bring me a *gut* man and the day after that *Mamm* started talking about Stephen. I knew he was the one for me."

Florence looked over at her stepmother who'd stayed silent all this time. That was what she did when things got difficult. Wilma didn't even see there was a problem, so Florence had to be the voice of reason. "I just don't want you to be disappointed, or feel you have to marry him because Ada and *Mamm* think you should."

Mamm looked down at the table and kept silent.

"No one's going to influence me. You'll see. Stephen and I will get along better than you've ever seen two people get along. We'll go together like pepper and salt, apple pie and ice-cream, peanut butter and jelly."

Florence looked down at her plate. "I hope so."

Then *Mamm* lifted her head. "Stop worrying so, Florence. *Gott* wants people to marry. It's His intention that everyone find someone."

"*Jah,*" Joy said, "In Proverbs it says,

Whoso findeth a wife findeth a good thing, and obtaineth favour of the Lord. It would be the same as for a woman. If you find a husband, Mercy, you'll be finding a good thing. Don't listen to Florence." Joy stared at Florence almost defiantly, and all *Mamm* did was smile.

"*Gut* girl, Joy," Wilma said, "You've been reading again."

"*Jah*. I have." Joy, the third oldest of Wilma's daughters, often quoted from the Bible and rarely let anyone get away with anything without telling them what the Word said.

Mercy, who was sitting next to Florence, looped her arm through hers. "And when I'm married, I'll find one of Stephen's older friends for you. We can all sit around the table having dinners together just the four of us."

Florence giggled and gave up her quest, for now. "That would be nice. And we'll all live close so things here will never have to change. We'll keep working on the orchard."

Mercy let go of Florence's arm and straightened in her chair. "I don't know if I'll stick around here. I'll have to go wherever my husband wants, and Stephen lives in Connecticut."

"*Jah,* she'll have to be an obedient wife," Joy added.

Florence ignored Joy. "Mercy, don't you think he'll willingly listen to your opinion and you'll decide together where you'll live?"

"I don't want you to move away," *Mamm* added somberly, as though she hadn't thought about that until now.

"I might not move, but I'll be out from this *haus.*" Mercy smiled. "Who'll miss me when I get married?"

"Everyone will," Honor said.

Hope added, "It'll be one less pair of hands around here."

Mercy's mouth turned down at the corners. "Is that all I am to you all? Just an extra pair of hands?"

"Sometimes," Florence said, "Especially when you're mean to me like you were this morning."

"I'm sorry."

"It's okay. I know how important your dress is to you. I'll start sewing again shortly and won't stop until it's done. Then I'll pin the hem for you."

"Denke, Florence. You're the best."

"I know. I'm the best older sister you'll ever have."

Mercy frowned. "What?"

"That's a joke, Mercy," Honor said.

Favor giggled, "Don't worry, Mercy."

Florence had forgotten that Mercy had no sense of humor.

Mamm pushed herself out of her chair and stood up. "Who's going to clean up in here while Florence sews? She can't do everything."

"I'll do it," Mercy said, "since Florence is finishing my dress."

"I'll help you," said Honor.

"*Gut*. And the rest of you girls can wash the floors, sweep the porch and pull weeds out of the front garden before our guests come tomorrow."

The younger girls groaned.

CHAPTER 5

Just before the Baker family's guests were due to arrive for dinner on Thursday night, Mercy waited in her upstairs bedroom. Wearing her new dress, she felt confident. With her palms, she smoothed her violet dress down enjoying how the fabric was cool and smooth against her fingertips. It was a nice change from the normal dark heavy fabric all their everyday dresses were made from. They'd worn clothes made from that material since they were young. To make matters worse, hers had all been Florence's hand-me-downs, and they went on down the line until they reached Cherish or were worn out.

Honor rushed into Mercy's bedroom. "They're here."

Mercy hurried to the window and looked out. From her window she could see from the house to the barn and beyond, with a clear view of who was coming and going.

Joy suddenly joined them in looking out the window. "Is that him?" asked Joy just as a young man stepped out of the buggy and looked around.

"*Jah* it is." Mercy's eyes were glued to her future husband examining his every movement.

"How do you know? You've never met him before."

"There's no one else coming. It must be him." Mercy stared at the tall and slim young man as he adjusted his hat and then straightened his jacket. He looked skinnier than most men, which wasn't too appealing, but she figured he'd fill out with the passing of time. "I think he's very handsome. He'll suit me nicely."

Joy giggled.

Mercy didn't care what anyone else thought. This was her decision to make and hers alone. "We'll marry before the end of the year." Mercy stared at him from the high bedroom window, watching him walk toward the house between his aunt and uncle.

"But what if he doesn't like you?" Honor asked.

"Of course he will. Why wouldn't he?" Mercy stared back and forth between her sisters.

Honor opened her mouth and ended up shaking her head instead. "I don't know."

"Just make sure no one chatters too much throughout the meal, and tell the others the same. I want him to be talking only to me. Okay?"

"Jah." Joy nodded. "You can talk as much as you want and we won't say anything."

"Don't make it weird. Just be normal. Tell the others."

"I wonder what Ada said about you?" Honor asked as the girls stared back at their guests.

"She would've said a lot of nice things."

Joy turned her attention to Mercy. "Your dress looks nice."

Mercy looked down at her dress. *"Jah,* it turned out good. You two stay here. I want to meet him first." Mercy left her sisters and hurried out of the bedroom to meet her future beloved.

WITH HER STEPMOTHER busy finishing off the gravy in the kitchen, Florence opened the front door and a ruddy-faced young man stepped forward. "Mrs. Baker, I've heard so much about you and your *dochders*. It's nice to meet you." He smiled and offered his hand.

Florence was devastated, although she did her best not to show it. He thought she was Wilma. Did she really look old enough to have six teenage daughters? Even if she'd married young and had a child at eighteen that would have to put her around thirty-six or thirty-seven, allowing for the nine months of pregnancy. Did this young man think she looked more than twelve years older than she actually was? It was an insult to the highest degree, but she could tell by the anxiousness in the poor young man's large green eyes that he was horribly nervous.

Ada stepped forward and filled in the silence. "This is Florence, Stephen. Mrs. Baker's step-*dochder.*" Florence hated how Ada emphasized the word "step."

His shoulders drooped and he stared sheepishly at Florence. "Oh, forgive me! I'm so sorry. I didn't even look at you very closely. You're obviously not old enough."

He wasn't the first person to think she was older than her years. She never gave much thought to her appearance, but every now and again she wondered what it would be like to have people—men—look at her the way they looked at Mercy. Florence laughed it off. "It's fine. Welcome. Come inside and meet everyone."

"I'm really, really sorry," he said as he took off his hat to reveal a mop of sandy-colored hair.

"Forget it. Here, I'll take that from you." She took Ada's coat and the men's hats and jackets, hanging them on pegs near the door. All the while Stephen kept apologizing.

"I don't know how I could've made such a mistake," he said once more.

Ada patted his shoulder soothingly as she said, "It was the light and the shadows. It's just on dark and the light plays tricks."

"It's easily done. Don't worry," Florence assured all of them. The more they went on about it the worse she felt.

Florence was saved by Wilma who hurried out of the kitchen to meet Stephen and greet her friends.

MEANWHILE, Mercy was halfway down the stairs when she saw Stephen. He looked up at her and their eyes locked. It was as though they both knew they were meant for one another. His gaze left hers when Ada introduced him to *Mamm*. Mercy hurried over to be included in the introductions.

As soon as she was close, her mother grabbed her arm and pulled her forward. "And this is my eldest, Mercy. That is if you don't count Florence, my step-*dochder*."

"Nice to meet you, Mercy. I'm Stephen Wilkes."

"Hello, Stephen." He was even more

handsome up close with his unusual green eyes, and he was tall.

"My other girls are around here somewhere. Upstairs most likely. They'll be down soon. Florence, take everyone through to the living room while Mercy and I finish off in the kitchen."

Florence did what she was asked, and when Mercy was alone in the kitchen with *Mamm,* she whispered, "What do you think, *Mamm?*"

"He looks like he'd match you nicely. I can see the two of you together. I can picture it in my mind."

"I knew it. And he was polite and everything and he's handsome too, don't you think, *Mamm?*"

"He is. Ada and even Samuel had good things to say about him, so I was expecting him to be well-suited. Ada hasn't ever let me down when making a recommendation."

CHAPTER 6

WHEN EVERYONE WAS GATHERED around the table and had said their prayers of thanks for the food, Samuel asked, "When does the fruit picking start?"

"On Monday," Florence said. "We've got lots of work to get through before then."

"Florence has arranged for the girls to bake pies and make a supply of other items for the shop." *Mamm* turned to Stephen and explained that at harvest time they sold goods from the small building that stood at the edge of their property alongside the road.

Year around, they had a roadside stall where they sold vegetables, jams, jellies, apple-butter, and pickles along with other goodies.

As Ada helped herself to some roast chicken, she said, "I told Stephen all about the store and what you sell there."

"It sounds interesting. I'd like to see it."

"There'll be taffy apples, applesauce, apple relish and butter, and of course the freshly pickled apples. Oh, and cider. Do you have use of a buggy while you're here, Stephen?" *Mamm* asked barely drawing a breath.

"I do. *Onkel* Samuel's allowing me the use of one of his."

Mamm leaned forward and stared at Stephen with her pale brown eyes nearly boring through him. "Perhaps you'd like Mercy to show you around tomorrow? That is, if you're not busy doing something else?"

"I'd like that." He gave Mercy a big smile. "What do you say, Mercy?"

"I'd be okay with that." Mercy was grateful her sisters didn't start giggling. She knew from their faces they were trying hard not to.

"Good. Shall I collect you at nine?" he asked.

"*Jah.* Perfect."

"Have you picked apples before, Stephen?" Hope asked, smiling.

"Not apples, but I've picked other fruit. I've traveled south to pick oranges with one of my brothers."

"It's quite hard work," Honor said.

He nodded. "Don't I know it. The first time I picked fruit I was about ten. It was the hardest work I'd done. Since then I've done a lot harder work. I've done all kinds. I've done construction, I helped out our blacksmith, and I've dug holes for fencing. I'm sure I'll be able to handle picking apples without too much bother."

"We have a race to see who can pick the

most buckets by the end of the day. We make a game out of it," Favor told him.

Florence frowned. "I don't like that *game* because there's a risk of the fruit being damaged by rough handling. The Honeycrisps are especially vulnerable to bruising, but we have customers who come back specifically for them every year. We can't sell damaged apples. Once they're bruised they'll go bad and contaminate the apples around them. We won't even be able to use them in the cider or the vinegar."

"I'll be careful. Do all you girls help out in the orchard?" Stephen asked, while looking directly at Mercy.

Cherish said, *"Mamm* doesn't allow me to go outside much."

"She misses out on the fun," Honor told the visitors. "She's spoiled." Honor giggled loudly and Mercy glared at her. She'd told them not to draw attention away from her, and talking about Cherish was doing just that.

Stephen didn't seem to notice what anyone was talking about because his gaze was firmly fixed on Mercy. When Mercy saw Stephen smiling at her, she looked down and cleared her throat. In an effort to show herself to be a good conversationalist, she then said, "We had trouble with cows in the orchard today."

"You have cows as well?" Stephen asked.

"*Nee*, they're from next door." Florence answered before Mercy had a chance. "*Mamm,* I haven't told you yet. We have a new neighbor, an *Englischer.*"

"The Graingers sold?" *Mamm* asked.

"*Jah.*"

"How did the cows get out?" Honor asked.

"The cows broke the fence down by pushing on a weak spot."

Mamm frowned as she buttered a piece of bread. "Did he fix it properly?"

"I had to help him. He seemed a bit useless. He's a city man."

Mamm sighed. "You would think they would've told us they were moving."

"Did the new neighbor bring the cows?" Samuel asked.

"Seems the Graingers left them there, almost like they were part of the barn." Florence giggled. "He didn't tell me so, but maybe he got there, ready to move in, and saw the cows. He mightn't even have known the Graingers were going to leave them."

Stephen cleared his throat. "That reminds me of a joke." Everyone looked at him, and he continued, "Who wants to hear it?"

Hope was quick to say, "I do."

"Jah, tell us a joke, Stephen," *Mamm* said, smiling.

"Why did the cow cross the road?"

"Why?" *Mamm* asked.

"To get to the *udder* side."

Everyone grinned or laughed except for Mercy.

"You mean to get to the *other* side," Mercy stated.

Hope, who was seated next to Mercy, dug her in the ribs. "It's a joke, Mercy. Get it? Udder—other?"

Mercy shook her head, unsure why everyone was laughing. He used a wrong word ... so, how was that funny?

"I've got another one." Stephen's face was beaming. "What would you call a cow when it's eating grass?" When everyone just looked at him, he gave the answer. "A lawn moo-er."

Once again everyone but Mercy laughed.

Then he told yet another. "Here's a good one. What do you call a sleeping bull?" He paused a moment. "A bull dozer."

Giggles rang out while Mercy sat in silence.

"Tell us more," Cherish said.

He shook his head. "I think that's enough, especially at dinner."

As soon as all was quiet. Mercy giggled, trying to please Stephen, and everyone looked at her.

"What are you laughing at?" Joy asked her. "No one said anything."

"Just the jokes." Then Mercy looked across the table at Stephen and they shared a secret smile.

CHAPTER 7

WHEN THE VISITORS LEFT, the five younger girls were sent to bed leaving Mercy in the kitchen with Florence and *Mamm*. "What did you think of him, Florence?" Mercy asked, anxious to know her sister's opinion.

"I think he's lovely. Very nice, but it's more important what you think of him."

"I'll still marry him even if I don't understand his jokes."

"And that's okay," *Mamm* said, "You don't have to understand him to have a happy marriage. Sometimes you don't want to marry someone too much like yourself. You'll have a lifetime to learn about him."

"You liked him too, *Mamm?*" Mercy asked.

"I did and it was clear how much he liked you."

Florence giggled. *"Jah,* it was because of the dress I sewed."

"Oh, Florence, the dress was good, but it was Mercy's personality and her pretty face he was drawn to."

"Er, I know that *Mamm,*" Florence said. It seemed Mercy wasn't the only one who didn't catch it when someone said something as a joke.

Mercy started clearing dishes off the table. "You have to say that just because you're my *mudder.*"

"I'm not telling fibs. It's true. Just don't get prideful."

Mercy sighed. "I won't. Tonight was okay because everyone else was around. What if we have nothing to talk about tomorrow? I'm a little nervous to be alone with him."

"Then you won't marry him and you'll find someone else who suits you better." Florence thought that was a perfectly normal thing to say, but Wilma didn't agree.

"Florence, if you don't have anything nice to say, don't say anything at all. You can see Mercy has her heart set on marrying Stephen."

"I know that, but surely she won't marry him if he's unsuitable."

"He will be suitable. I mean, he is. Ada said he's perfectly fine and she recommends him. She's known him since he was a little *bu*."

Florence shook her head. "Okay. I'll keep out of it then."

"Good. I think Mercy was talking to me anyway, not you."

"*Nee, Mamm,* I'm interested in what Florence has to say because she's sensible."

Florence was pleased Mercy was willing to listen to her advice. "We can talk later, Mercy. Why don't you two talk in the living room while I clean up in here?"

Mamm nodded and then Mercy said, "You can't do all this by yourself, Florence. And you've got the store to clean tomorrow."

"It won't be much work. I'll just be doing a bit of this and that. It won't be too hard."

"Nee, I'll help you in here. You go to bed, *Mamm.* I'll bring you up a nice hot cup of tea."

"You're so sweet, Mercy. I'd really like that."

When their mother was gone, Mercy made and delivered the tea. Then she helped Florence finish clearing the dishes. There was a large area off from the kitchen with a table that seated twelve. It was where they ate all their meals.

"I'm pleased *Mamm* likes him and I know you're cautious. I'm stuck between the two of you." She giggled. "I'll find out more about him tomorrow and then I'll make my final decision. Now that she's gone, you can tell me what you really think about Stephen."

Florence gathered the dishes and walked them over to the sink ready for washing, and while she walked, she said, "I *really think* he's very nice from what we've seen of him tonight, but you have to really get to know a person. You just can't go on meeting them once. Everyone is on their best behavior when they're meeting someone for the first time. You ought to see him in different situations. See how he interacts with his family and his friends. See him in different stressful situations to know how he acts in a crisis."

Mercy stared at her. "You've really got finding a husband all figured out."

Florence laughed. "If that were true, I'd be married by now."

"You've been thinking a lot about it. You must've been. I mean, look how old you are.

Haven't you been thinking and hoping you'll marry?"

"I do like to daydream."

"So, you do want to get married?"

"I do. I never said I didn't."

"That's good."

Five minutes later, when the plates were rinsed and stacked and ready to be washed, Mercy said, in almost a whisper, "You'll find someone, Florence. Someday, someone will come for you."

"I know it," Florence said, wanting to sound positive, because deep down that was her secret hope. The Bible talked a lot about hope and it was important to have some. If she hoped, it would increase her faith and God might reward her with the desires of her heart.

WHEN FLORENCE WAS in bed that night she tossed and turned; she couldn't stop thinking about love. Mercy had said someone would come for her and just as those words echoed in her mind, an image of the neighbor next door jumped into Florence's mind. He wasn't the strong Amish man that God had for her somewhere, but she had been attracted to him and she'd never had those feelings before. It made sense he was a sign for her, sent from God. A sign not to give up and that there *was* someone for her. Florence fell asleep comforted that she wouldn't be alone forever.

CHAPTER 8

ON FRIDAY MORNING, Mercy was so nervous about going out with Stephen that she knew she'd have to force herself to eat breakfast. Her younger sisters weren't helping matters with their constant chatter while they waited for Florence to finish cooking the pancakes.

"What will you talk about with him?" Honor, the next-younger sister, asked just as Mercy sipped hot black tea with a little mint added to settle her tummy.

That was the very thing Mercy was worried about, but she wasn't going to admit it to any of her sisters. "I don't know. Whatever he wants to talk about, I guess."

"Now it's time for our prayer of thanks," Florence announced. She was always the one to tell the girls what to do while their mother sat there, almost unaware of what was going on.

They all bowed their heads and each said a silent prayer the same way they did before they began every meal. As soon as they had all opened their eyes, the questions for Mercy started again. This time it was Cherish's turn. "Where are you going with him?"

"I'm not sure yet. I suppose I'll have to—"

Honor interrupted, "Don't you think you should plan what you're going to say? That's what I'd do. That time I had to stand in front of the class and say what we did the weekend just gone, I had to plan it a little—otherwise I would've stood there not knowing what to say."

Mamm said, "That was years ago."

"It's still on my mind."

"*Nee,* Honor, I'll let the conversation flow naturally. You're making me nervous. Zip your lips."

The other sisters giggled and even *Mamm's* mouth turned upward.

Honor didn't find it funny. "But what if it doesn't flow? He didn't say much last night. All he did was tell those dreadful jokes."

"That will be enough," *Mamm* reprimanded her.

"They weren't dreadful. You're saying that because you have no sense of humor," Florence said. "Anyway, I saw you laughing too."

"I didn't laugh, and neither did she." Cherish pointed at Mercy.

"Cherish, go to your room now," Florence said.

"Do I have to, *Mamm?*"

When *Mamm* just sat there, Florence said, "One thing *Dat* always disliked was people saying rude things about others. I won't have it in this *haus*."

"You're right, Florence. You'd better go to your room, Cherish."

Cherish looked horrified. This was probably the first time *Mamm* had agreed with Florence about punishing her. Normally, Cherish could do no wrong in *Mamm's* eyes. She stood up and knocked her chair over in the process. Florence, who'd been sitting next to her, picked it up while Cherish picked up the bottom of her dress in both fists and strode out of the room. They all sat in silence listening to her stomping up the stairs.

"That girl's got a temper. I don't know where she gets it," *Mamm* said shaking her head.

"From the devil." Everyone gasped at Joy's words. Joy was taken aback by their reactions. "I'm sorry, but where else would she get the temper? All good things come from

Gott, so where else but the devil do you think the other things come from?"

Florence shifted uncomfortably in her chair. It wasn't the pleasant start to the day for which she'd hoped. In her experience, the breakfast always set the tone for the girls for the remainder of the day. "Let's just eat, shall we?"

They ate the rest of their meal in silence, Mercy's nerves apparent as she picked at her pancakes.

AN HOUR LATER, Mercy was pretty much done getting ready when she looked out the window and saw Stephen coming up the driveway. She couldn't wait to get away from the house. She finished tying the strings of her prayer *kapp* and then took hold of her black shawl, raced out the bedroom door and ran down the stairs taking them two at a time. "Bye," she called out to everyone before she pulled open the front door. When she stepped out into the daylight, Stephen was out of his buggy and heading toward the house.

"How are you this fine morning?" His face beamed with a smile.

"I'm good. And, how are you?"

"Great. I'm just going to say hello to everyone before we start."

"No need. They're all busy anyway."

He looked up at the house. "Are you sure?"

"*Jah*. Come on." She started walking toward the buggy hoping he'd follow and he did.

"Where are we going?" he asked.

"Where would you like to go?"

He smiled at her and repeated, "Where would *you* like to go?"

Then she remembered what her mother

had said over dinner. "Would you like me to show you the town?"

"I'd like that."

"Okay, let's go."

Before they had a chance to get into the buggy her sister's dog ran at Stephen and jumped up at him.

"Stop it, Caramel! I'm so sorry. This is my sister's dog and she hasn't bothered to train him."

Stephen laughed, crouched down and gave the dog a few pats. "It's okay. I love dogs. I've got Buster. He looks a little similar to this one, but he's bigger. I miss him already. I had him since he was six weeks old. I could hold him in the palm of my hand. Caramel's an unusual name."

"It's Cherish's dog. She loves candy and caramel is her favorite flavor. It's a dumb name I know."

Cherish came running out of the house.

"There he is. I'm sorry." She grabbed Caramel's collar and then picked him up.

"Train him," Mercy said.

"He is trained. He can sit."

"Yeah, well train him to come to you, *jah?*"

Cherish simply frowned at her and walked away with the dog.

Mercy told Stephen, "She's the youngest and a little bit spoiled. She wasn't well when she was younger and that's when she got the dog. That's a whole other story."

"It must've worked for her. I hope Buster's not missing me too much."

"I'm sure he'll be fine. Let's go." Mercy walked over to the buggy and Stephen followed.

CHAPTER 9

AFTER MERCY HAD LEFT on her important date with Stephen, Florence escaped to her sanctuary, the log cabin shop her father had built close to the road.

Florence placed the large black key in the lock and turned it to the left. This would be the first time she'd been in the place for many months. It'd only need one day to give it a good cleaning and she much preferred to do that away from her giggling noisy sisters. Pushing open the door, she inhaled the aroma of wood mixed with the sweet smell of beeswax from the candles she'd lit at dusk to add up the takings on the last day she had worked there—several months ago.

Soon the place would be bustling with tourists, as well as locals who came back every year for the fresh apple pies, pickles and chutneys. The shelves were already stocked with jarred and canned goods and the boxed crates of apple cider vinegar bottles were full to the brim. They'd need more as the season progressed but with this supply it was a good start.

The place would need a good dusting and then everything would have to be washed down. Realizing she'd forgotten her cleaning items, she spun around intending to fetch them when she faced a large silhouette in the doorway. She gasped in fright at the unexpected sight.

It was Carter from next door. "You want to inspect the fence?" he asked.

Her hand moved to her chest. "You scared

me half to death. What were you doing sneaking up on me?"

"You said you'd be here."

"Did I?" She couldn't recall she'd told him anything of the kind.

"How are your hands today?"

She looked down at them. "Much better thanks. Good enough for me to use them today."

"That's great to hear. Do you want to inspect the fence? I strengthened it."

"I'm sure it's fine. As long as it keeps the cows out of the orchard, it'll be good enough."

"It will, but I wanted to show it to you to get your feedback. This is the first fence I've ever repaired."

She didn't have time to waste today. "I'm sure it'll be fine, and I'm busy at the moment."

"With what?"

"Trying to get the store ready. If you don't

mind, I've got a lot of work to do and I work best when I'm alone." She was surprised when she heard herself sound so abrupt, but he didn't seem to notice.

He walked further into the shop. "It's not much fun being alone."

Fun? She couldn't remember the last time she'd had anything that resembled fun. Not with all her responsibilities. This man obviously didn't have a care in the world and for some reason that irritated her. "I don't want to look at the fence. Just keep the cows out next time, okay? Then we can live in peace next door to each other."

He didn't seem to notice her irritation as he walked over and picked up a bottle of apple cider vinegar. He read out the label, and then asked, "What do people use this for?"

"It's apple cider vinegar."

"I know that. I can read even though I'm

not good with cows. What do people *use* it for?"

"A lot of women buy it for beauty products. It's good for the hair and skin, they tell me."

"Putting it on the outside or drinking it?"

"Both. It also helps to ward off colds and has many other health benefits. Too many to name, and possibly more too that no one's discovered yet." She reached under the countertop and pulled out a leaflet. "Here. Read this." He stood there looking it over. "You can keep it. Take it with you,"

"Thanks." He put the bottle back, folded the leaflet and slipped it into the back pocket of his jeans, and then dusted off his hands. He looked at her and then nodded to the bottles of vinegar. "You might want to dust those."

"I'm getting to that. Come back on Monday and the whole place will be spotless. That's when we're officially open."

"Am I annoying you?"

"I've only got one day to clean this place. So, to answer your question, you're not annoying me, but you are in my way."

He laughed. "I like an honest woman."

"I hope you find one. There must be another one out there somewhere."

He frowned at her. "I'm sorry."

She stepped out from behind the counter. "For what?"

"For wasting your time. I won't do it again." She stared at him and he raised both hands, palms facing her. "Okay, I know when I'm not wanted." He walked out of the one-room building and she was glad.

It took a few seconds for her to regret her rudeness, but by then it was too late. Stepping out the door, she looked for him. When she spotted him, he was a tiny figure in the distance disappearing behind a clump of trees. "At least you won't bother me again," she muttered under her breath.

She walked back to the house and saw some of her sisters were still there and they hadn't begun collecting the apples from the ground. "Who's working the stall today?"

"You didn't tell us we were doing the stall."

"We do the stall every day. We can't afford to lose the money we make." Florence could feel her heart rate gallop as she tried to keep calm. "Joy and Honor can do the stall and they better hurry. Hope, gather the girls and tell them what's happening. Favor and Cherish can start getting those apples together, *jah?*"

Hope shrugged her shoulders as she sat on the couch staring into space holding onto a white coffee mug. "It won't take long. We'll do it later."

"*Jah,* we'll do it when Mercy comes back," said Honor, who was sitting on the opposite couch. "Why should I work the stall when Mercy has a day off. That's why I thought we weren't doing the stall today, Florence. You didn't say who was going to replace Mercy."

"Can't anyone around here think for themselves?" Florence yelled.

Mamm came rushing out of the kitchen. "Florence, what's wrong?"

"No one's organized the stall. Just because Mercy has a day off everyone thinks they can have one."

"*Jah,* well they can't, can they?"

"*Nee, Mamm.* They need to move now and get that wagon to the road and set up that stall!" Florence put her hand over her chest and felt her heart pumping. She was so angry with everyone.

Mamm licked her lips and looked at the girls lazing on the couch. "All of you do what Florence tells you."

Florence knew it was hard for *Mamm* to say that and she was grateful. "I don't care who does it but two of you need to set up that stall and get moving NOW!"

Joy fixed her eyes on her. "What are *you* going to do?"

"I'm cleaning out the store and it'll take me all day. We talked about this last night."

"Do what she says, girls. Joy and Honor, you do the stall today."

"I'll finish my *kaffe*," Joy said.

"*Nee* you won't!" *Mamm* told her. "You're already late, so you'll go without. Set it down now and get in that wagon."

Her stepmother backing Florence up took a lot of pressure off her shoulders.

Begrudgingly, the two girls stood and started moving. Florence didn't wait to see what happened next. She headed to the back of the house to collect the mop, bucket and the cleaning rags while hoping *Mamm* would keep the pressure on the girls to do what they were asked. They had a way of getting out of things—if they whined persistently enough *Mamm* often gave in to them rather than disciplining them.

As she walked back to the store, the girls were hurrying to get the horse hitched to the wagon. The wagon was already pre-loaded with the goods for the roadside stall.

Once she was back in the store, Florence took a deep breath in and let it out slowly, slowly, relishing the silence. *Refrigerator first, or shelves? Hmmm ... shelves, I think.* She started from the top and worked down, wiping the jars as she took them off the shelves, and then scrubbing the wooden shelves until the rinsed rag came up clean.

When she was on the second shelf, her mind drifted to Mercy and she hoped she was having a good time getting to know Stephen. The last thing she wanted was for her sister to get into a bad marriage, but Mercy and Stephen seemed like a good match, and that had surprised her. It had always been the Amish way to marry young, and she knew that was what Mercy wanted.

CHAPTER 10

"How do you like it here so far?" Mercy smiled at Stephen as he drove the buggy.

He momentarily drew his eyes away from the road. "I like it here—a lot."

She felt all aglow when he smiled at her the way he had just now. He was even more handsome when he smiled.

"Aunt Ada said I should come here not only to help with picking the apples but also to meet you."

It was just as she'd thought. He had come to dinner knowing it was all a setup. The first thing she'd tell Florence when she got home was that she had been right and Florence was wrong. "Did she say that?"

He nodded and then turned his attention back to the road. "Ada likes you. She likes you a lot."

"My *mudder* and Ada are best friends. I think they've been best friends forever."

"The last time I was here I was five. I came with my whole family for my grandfather's funeral."

"That would be too far back for me to remember anything."

"Me too. I barely recall it. Mostly just so many people that I didn't know."

They traveled along the quiet country road in silence for a few minutes. She hoped he liked the area and the community enough to stay here after they married. Then she could be around her family rather than a bunch of people she'd have to get to know.

"I'm pleased you like it here." She

couldn't think of anything to say and she regretted not listening to Honor's advice.

"I like it a lot," he repeated the same thing he'd said earlier.

"That's good. And you'll get to meet everybody on Sunday and everybody is so nice."

"Good. I'm looking forward to it."

"Do you think you might like to maybe live here one day?"

"It's not totally out of the question. The community I come from is very small. I prefer to be around more people. That way it's livelier, and there'd be more things to do and more folks to visit."

Mercy smiled, imagining them with a large family. She wondered if he would talk about marriage today or whether it would take him a little longer. They both knew that was why he was there even though neither of them had said the word 'marriage.'

"Did you have breakfast?" she asked.

"Sure did. Ada filled me up with pancakes and some kind of sausage with a white cheese sauce."

"Oh, that sounds interesting. I'll have to get the recipe from her. I love cooking."

"Are you a good cook?"

"I like to think so. I do most of the cooking at home so obviously you'd have to ask the family how good I am."

"If they keep letting you back into the kitchen, you cannot be too bad." He laughed. "Have you ever traveled around to other communities?"

She shook her head. *"Nee.* Oh, we did a little before *Dat* died. We went to a few of our cousins' weddings and things like that but after he died we haven't been anywhere. We're too busy with the orchard and *Mamm* says it's too much trouble to go anywhere."

"I imagine that would keep you busy."

"I know a place that makes nice food."

"Around here?"

"Not too far.

"Maybe we could go there for lunch. If you can stay with me for that long?"

She was pleased he wanted to spend more than a couple of hours with her. "I can. I have the whole day free from chores and from the stall. I normally do Fridays on the stall but I got out of it today."

"Good. Your family is nice for letting you off your chores to spend the day with me."

"Of course they would. They like you. Especially after all the nice things Ada said about you."

"So, Ada did talk about me?" he asked.

"Of course. Is there anything that I should know about you that she wouldn't know?"

"Nothing that I can think of. I haven't done anything bad." He looked over at her and asked, "Have you?"

She put a hand up to her mouth and giggled. "Sometimes I tell one of my little sisters it's their turn to wipe the dishes and they can't remember whether it is so they do it anyway."

He gasped. "That's very wicked."

She felt dreadful. "Do you think so?"

He laughed. "Relax. I'm only joking."

"Oh." She giggled.

"Your secret's safe with me. I hope you're not going to be awful like that with me."

"If I knew you thought it was awful I wouldn't have confessed just now."

"Hmm. Smart as well as pretty." He glanced over at her and she felt the heat rise in her cheeks. "You must have a lot of men stopping by the house to see you."

"I don't." She shook her head vigorously hoping he didn't think he'd have to wait to marry her or be in competition with anybody else. "There's no one else, truly."

"I find that very hard to believe."

"It's true. It's totally true."

"You're the prettiest girl I've seen since

… Well, since forever."

"That can't be right." She giggled with embarrassment and also a small amount of delight.

"It is. I wouldn't lie. I'm blessed you're going out with me today. I know looks aren't everything and it's what's inside that counts, but it's *wunderbaar* when you can have both in one woman. Are you with me today just because your mother asked you to last night?"

"*Nee.* I wanted to go out with you."

"You did?"

"*Jah.*" She looked up at the road ahead. "Now turn left at this intersection."

"Yes ma'am. Where are we going?"

"Keep going along here. I'm taking you to a covered bridge. We've several of them around here and this one is really pretty and the trees are so nice. And the stream that runs alongside it is so nice at this time of year."

"Good. Then can we stop the buggy and take a little walk?"

"Sure, if you'd like to."

He leaned forward and looked up at the sky. "It's a beautiful day. And I love to walk."

"Do you?"

He nodded. "I do."

"I love how the sky looks this time of year."

"Me too."

"The trees are all kinds of colors. So pretty."

"I've got some jokes about trees. Do you want to hear 'em?"

She didn't, but she had to be polite if she wanted him to like her. "Sure, go ahead."

"Did you know I'm so good at cutting down trees I can do it just by looking at them?"

She frowned at him, wondering what she was supposed to say.

Then he said, "I *saw* them with my own eyes."

She had to be honest. "If that's a joke I don't get it."

"I *saw* them with my own eyes. Get it? Saw. You cut down trees with a saw." When she shook her head, he said, "I'll have to work on my delivery. It was a tricky one. How about this one? What kind of tree can you fit in your hand?"

"A very small one?"

"No. A palm tree." He chuckled.

"I don't understand that. You couldn't fit it in your hand if it was a large palm tree, but you could fit any young tree in your hand if it was small enough."

He drew his eyebrows together and lifted up his hand. "Palm and palm tree. It's a kind of a play on words."

"I see. I realize that. It just doesn't work." Even with his jokes she liked being with him.

"Okay, last one of the day. I'm sure you'll

think this one's funny. How do you know if a tree is a dogwood tree?"

"I don't know."

"By the bark." He laughed. "Get it?"

"*Jah,* I do. Dogs bark and trees have bark." She forced a giggle and that seemed to make him happy. Thankfully, he'd said it was the last joke of the day. A few miles along they drove around a bend and there it was— the bridge. "There, what do you think of it? It's very old. I'm sure there's a story attached to it somewhere, but I don't know it."

"It is indeed lovely. We could make up our own story about it."

A giggle escaped her lips at the look of wonder on his face. "We can drive through it and then to the left is a parking area and there just might even be a walking trail."

"Do you happen to know there's a trail for certain?"

"You'll have to wait and see."

"You haven't taken another man here,

have you?"

She gasped at the idea. "Oh no. You're the first man I've ever been alone with in a buggy."

He shook his head. "I still can't believe you haven't got men knocking on your door every single day."

She loved his attention and the constant compliments he gave. It was a magical moment as they drove through the darkness of the covered bridge and came through into the bright sunlight on the other side. With slight pressure on the reins, he moved the buggy off the road and into the parking area. Once he had stopped the buggy, they both jumped out at the same time and then he secured his horse.

"I can see a path," he said when he walked over to join her.

"Let's go." Feeling playful, she started running toward the trail and he ran after her.

"Wait for me," he called out.

CHAPTER 11

WHEN FLORENCE HAD FINISHED MOST of her cleaning, she regretted how rude she'd been to Carter. Hoping to make it up to him, she bundled together some canned apples into a box along with two bottles of apple cider vinegar. She looked around the store and was happy with how much she'd gotten done already. All she had left was to mop the floor and then it would be ready for the grand opening on Monday.

Several minutes later, after she'd picked some apples from one of the trees, she knocked on Carter's door holding the box of goodies close to herself. The door was slightly open and she found it strange when he didn't answer. His SUV was there so she knew he was home. She walked over to the window and saw him on the couch with a computer in his lap and earphones in his ears. His head was bobbing up and down like he was listening to music.

She contemplated leaving the goods by the front door but she wanted to apologize in person, so holding the box in one hand she tapped on the window with the other.

He looked up and she gave him a wave. He pulled out his earphones, set his computer down on the coffee table and leaped to his feet. He met her at the door, clean shaven and looking far more handsome than she remembered.

"This is a surprise and an unexpected one. Did you get all your work done?" he asked.

She resisted the temptation to tell him that surprises generally *were* unexpected and that was the nature of them. "Most of it, yes. I said I'd bring you some apples and here they are." She held the box out to him. "And I brought you some of the apple cider vinegar you seemed so intrigued about."

"That's very kind of you. How much do I owe you?"

She laughed. "Nothing of course."

"I have to give you something."

"No you don't."

He pulled a wallet out of his back pocket, opened it, pulled out a hundred dollar bill and held it out to her. "Take it."

"No!" She leaned back. "I just came here to—"

"Take it."

"No, I won't. It's a gift."

He shook his head while placing the money back in his wallet. As he did so she noticed he had many other notes in his wallet and they all looked like the first one. While he shoved it in his back pocket, he stepped back slightly. "Come in."

"I shouldn't. I've still got some work to do back at the shop."

"Surely you can have a five-minute break? Come in and I'll show you what I've done with this old place."

Just to be neighborly, she agreed. "All right, just for a couple of minutes. What were you doing just now?"

"Playing chess."

"Oh, that's right. Playing chess by yourself against the computer."

He frowned a little. "That's right."

She looked around the sparsely furnished place. The walls were blue at the top and the bottom half of the walls were covered with varnished wooden boards. In one corner of the room was a staircase. There was a small table with a single chair in one area of the L-shaped room and one two-seater couch and one coffee table in the other. A small TV sat on a wooden crate. The impression was the house of a person without much money, but then there was his car and what looked like an abundance of cash. She spun around to face him. "What is it you do when you're not playing chess?"

He laughed. "I know you think I'm just some lazy person who's not good with cows and sits on his computer all day, but Amish people aren't the only ones who work hard."

"I wasn't saying that."

His lips widened into a grin. "Come here."

She followed him through to the kitchen. It looked like a bomb had exploded and smelled stale—like years of dust had been unearthed. "This is a kitchen?"

"It was once. I've taken the cabinetry out and I'm about to redo it. There was a lot of wood and a lot of blue and the layout was wrong. All the cupboards were blue. The same shade as the living room."

She'd been there before when she was young and it looked a lot smaller than she'd remembered. "How long will it take for you to build a new kitchen?"

"I'm not going to do the actual construction of it. I've got others doing it. I was pleased with myself for taking the old one out. I thought you'd be impressed."

She couldn't help smiling. "You want to impress me?"

"Only to make up for the cows."

"Yes, I'm not happy about the cows. Which reminds me, what are you going to do with the cows?"

"In what way?"

"Do you intend to keep them here forever or will you send them to the butcher?"

He frowned at her and rubbed his chin. "Eat them?"

Then she remembered he knew nothing about farming. "They're not dairy cows."

"Do I have to *do* something with them?" He leaned against the wall. "Can't they just stay here to eat the grass and do what they please?"

"You want to keep them as pets?" She giggled not expecting his next answer.

"Yes." When she kept laughing, he added, "Is there a law against it?"

"No, but it's crazy." She stared at him and wondered how this chess-playing man who lived alone ran his life. "Most people have a cat or a dog if they want a pet. They're much easier. They're also smaller and far less trouble. You don't have to worry about fences so much." When he shook his head, she asked, "A guinea pig or a bird?"

He shook his head once more. "A dog would be the best choice."

"Yes, good. Get a dog. Leave cows to farmers."

Raising his eyebrows, he asked, "What pets do you have?"

He was trying to draw her into conversation, but she had to get back to the shop. That floor wasn't going to wash itself. She inched toward the door. "We have two cats that live in the barn. They sleep all day and they're not very friendly at all. One of my sisters has a small dog. It was supposed to be a golden lab but it never grew. I'm not sure what kind of dog it is. A mixed breed of sorts."

"You have no pets yourself?" he asked.

"I guess my trees are my pets."

He laughed. "You're an extraordinary woman."

She didn't know how to take that but decided he didn't mean it in a flattering way. "Have you done any other work on the house?" she asked walking to the door.

"I have. I've pulled out the bathroom too.

Come back in a few days to check on my progress if you like."

"When will it be finished?"

"I'm not sure. I figured I might paint the place too."

"Sure, I'll come back and have a look … someday." She backed away. "Enjoy your apples." She misjudged where the doorway of the kitchen was and bumped into a wall.

She was shocked and embarrassed—even more so when he smiled at her. "Careful, this is a construction site."

"More like a de-struction site."

He chuckled and sent tingles through her when he put his hand on her shoulder. "Let me walk you out before you do some real damage." When they were at the front door, he said, "Thanks again for your generosity."

"You're welcome."

"And you said the store will be open on Monday?"

"That's right."

"I might have to sample some of your apple pies."

She gave him a smile. "I might see you then … then." After that, she hurried away. She didn't want him to come back to the store. Neither did she want to bring him a pie since that would mean she'd have to see him again. The best thing she could do was to keep away from him completely.

When she was halfway through the orchard, she suddenly came to a halt when she realized he'd never answered her question about what he did. She resumed walking and to keep him out of her mind she thought about all they had to do the next day. It was going to be their busiest cooking day of the year.

CHAPTER 12

MEANWHILE, Stephen had caught up with Mercy and they were ambling along the walking trail while autumn leaves gently fell about them.

Stephen had been doing most of the talking, so now it was her turn. "When I get married and have my own *haus* I'm going to have my bedroom on the top floor where I can see the whole countryside. It'll be built on a hill. My bedroom now is above the doorway and I can see everything from there."

He gave her a big smile. "That's what I want."

"And when I have that home, I'm going to open all the blinds during the day. *Mamm* prefers the place dark and for every blind to be pulled down. It's always so gloomy and depressing. I think the light makes me happy."

"I like a well-lit *haus* too."

She giggled. "We have a lot in common."

"I didn't notice your place was so dark. I guess that's because I was there at night."

Mercy sighed. "The only sunlight comes from the living room, the window in front of Florence's sewing machine. The machine was her mother's and that's the only one we have. If she won't allow us to use it we have to hand-sew everything." Florence had so many privileges that it annoyed Mercy most of the time. *Mamm* always allowed Florence to do whatever she liked. It was normally Florence who reprimanded them while *Mamm* sat there without saying a word.

"She won't allow you to use it?"

"She does, when she feels like it and only when she's not sewing."

"Is sewing by hand that bad?" Stephen inquired.

"*Nee.* I don't mind it. It's just that sometimes it's so much quicker to use the machine. Especially for doing long straight seams." When she thought he looked bored, she tried to think of something interesting to say. "Are you getting a little hungry yet?"

He smiled. "A little."

"We should go to the diner I was telling you about."

"Okay."

"Let's go back."

They spun around and started their way back to the buggy. Just as they did, a breeze swept up through the trees and sent a flurry of golden leaves down on them.

SAMANTHA PRICE

WHEN THEY REACHED THE DINER, Mercy told Stephen she was too nervous to sit inside amongst the *Englischers* who might stare at her.

Stephen shrugged agreeably. "So, what do you want to eat?"

"Their fried chicken is *wunderbaar*. It's their signature dish."

"Sounds great to me," Stephen said with a grin, heading inside to buy take-out for them.

When he returned with a bag full of delicious smells, they drove back and found a spot by the river. They sat at a table eating fried chicken, creamy coleslaw, and fresh-baked rolls while admiring the water.

Stephen was perfect for her, Mercy mused, except for his jokes. She had never understood jokes and didn't see why people thought such things were funny. It bothered her a little but not enough to stop her marrying him. Everything else about him appealed to her and she hoped he felt the same about her.

ON THE WAY back home in the buggy, Stephen let out a yell that made her jump.

"What is it?"

"That man walking up ahead—I know him. That's my brother."

She turned to see an Amish man with a knapsack slung casually over his shoulder.

Stephen pulled the buggy over to one side and jumped out. The young men spoke for a moment and then she watched them both heading back to the buggy. They were similar in appearance except for his brother being a little taller and not quite as thin, and—she guessed—a little older. Stephen then introduced his brother, Jonathon, who wore a big smile. Stephen got into the buggy while Jonathon, still on the ground outside the buggy, shook Mercy's hand.

"Pleased to meet you, Mercy."

"It's nice to meet you, too. This is a surprise. I certainly wasn't expecting to meet Stephen's brother today."

He jumped in the back and then leaned over and said to Stephen. "And this is the woman Aunt Ada's been talking about at such great length?" Stephen laughed, and then Jonathon told Mercy, "I'm here to help with picking the apples. Aunt Ada made it sound exciting and I didn't want Stephen to have all the fun. I'm going to work for free."

"Me too," said Stephen. "I couldn't take money from you, Mercy, or your family."

"*Nee,* you must. *Mamm* won't allow anyone to work for nothing. Only the local families who help us every year, but we supply them with apples. All the other workers will be paid. *Mamm* won't like it any other way."

"I'll talk her into it. I have a way of getting everything I want."

"It's true. He does," Stephen admitted. "And, *bruder* Jonathon, were you hitchhiking?"

"There's nothing wrong with that. It's the easiest way to get around."

"I'm sorry for this interruption to our day, Mercy," Stephen said.

"She won't be sorry. You're probably boring and tedious. Now I'm here to liven things up."

Stephen smiled as he moved his horse forward. "One thing you'll learn after you get to know my brother is, never believe a thing he says."

"I see I came just in time before you spread rumors about me."

"They aren't rumors if they're true."

Mercy stayed quiet, unsure of what to say

while the brothers' banter went back and forth. She guessed they were teasing, but that was as incomprehensible to her as Stephen's jokes had been. When they got to her house she stepped down from the buggy. "Goodbye, Jonathon."

"See you around, Mercy."

Stephen was quick to get out of the buggy. "I'll walk you in."

"Denke."

Then Jonathon got out, and said, "I'll come in and meet everyone. I'll tell your *Mamm* I'm working for free."

Stephen turned around. "Not today, Jonathon. They've had a busy day. You can meet them all at the meeting on Sunday."

"Okay." He didn't seem to mind and slipped into the driver's seat.

When they were away from the buggy a little ways, Stephen said, "I'm really sorry our day out was ruined. Well, the end of it was."

"*Nee,* it wasn't ruined. Just interrupted. I had a good day. It was the best one I've ever had in my whole entire life, in all my born days." She smiled at him. The day *had* been ruined by his brother, but she wouldn't tell Stephen so. They'd missed out on talking privately in those last fifteen minutes. In her daydreams, he'd proposed within days and she had secretly hoped he would have done so today.

"Me too. Does that mean you'll come out again with me sometime?"

"I'd like that."

"Can I see you tomorrow?"

She stopped walking and he stopped too and faced her. *"Nee. Mamm* will have a heart attack and so will Florence. We have to spend the whole day making apple pies and things for the shop."

"All of you? Won't that be a little crowded in the kitchen?"

"Yeah, it will, but if I'm not doing that

she'll have other things for me to do." She saw from his downturned mouth how upset he was. "I had a really good time today."

"Me too. You won't change your mind about going out with me again, will you?"

"I won't." When she stared into his eyes, peace and fulfilment welled within her. This was the man she was going to marry and she knew it. "I'll see you on Sunday, Stephen."

"I won't be able to wait."

She giggled. "Me either. Bye, Stephen."

"Bye, Mercy." She hurried to the house while he walked back to the buggy.

CHAPTER 13

WHEN FLORENCE HAD FINISHED WASHING the floor of the shop, she walked back to the house with the mop and bucket in one hand, and all the other cleaning equipment in a basket on her opposite hip. When she was still a distance from the house, she smelled dinner cooking and remembered she'd forgotten to eat lunch. It seemed if she didn't organize things, even things as simple as a meal, no one else bothered.

Mercy ran out of the house to meet her. "You'll never guess what happened today."

"He proposed already?" Florence asked teasing her.

"*Nee*. His *bruder*, Jonathon, is here too, and he's helping us with the harvest."

"*Gut*. Many hands make the load lighter. Have you met him?"

"I did. Stephen wasn't even expecting him. We caught up to him walking along the road when we were coming back here. He'd been hitchhiking to Ada and Samuel's. He said he'd work for free, and then Stephen said he's doing the same."

"*Ach, nee*. I won't hear of that. We always pay our workers."

"I know. We're not taking handouts because we're not in need, and I told them so. I'm just telling you what he said."

"What's he like?"

"He seems nice. He's older than Stephen and nearly as handsome." Mercy took the basket of cleaning items from Florence as they continued toward the house.

"*Denke.* I'm happy you get along with Stephen. It was just like you thought."

"I know. I told you he's the right man for me. And, he did know he was coming here specifically to meet me, like I thought—no truth to your worry about a secret conspiracy."

DURING THEIR DINNER of pork chops, mashed potatoes, beets, carrots, and asparagus, Honor asked Mercy about her date. The girls were excited because Mercy was the first of the girls to go anywhere alone with a man. "Did you find enough to talk with him about, Mercy?"

"It was hard at first, and I remember thinking, I wish I'd listened to Honor, and then we just started talking about anything and everything. He's so easy to talk with."

"*Gut.*"

"We talked about seventy things at least. And I really like him. He's nice and he's kind and … and he stopped joking after a while."

"Just ask him to stop joking," Joy told her.

"I don't know about that," said Florence. "She could hurt his feelings if she did that."

Mercy bit her lip. "I don't want to do that."

"Is it something you can't look past?" *Mamm* asked.

"It doesn't bother me."

Honor leaned closer to Mercy. "Would you marry him if he asked you?"

"Of course I will, and I'm sure he'll ask me. I just don't know when."

"After dinner, Florence has organized for us to stew the apples so they're ready for to-morrow's pie baking," Honor told Mercy.

"I never get a chance to roll out the pas-try. Can you show me how to do that tomor-row, *Mamm?*" asked Joy.

"Okay. I've shown you all how to do it before, but I'll show you again."

"Then what will I do?" Honor asked.

"There'll be plenty for us all to do."

Florence could sense some arguments brewing in the air. "I'll make up a timetable and assign each of us some chores in a rotation."

"As long as it's fair," Joy said with a pout.

"Everyone will have equal work and get to do a bit of everything, and that way it'll be fair, plus it will help us keep on track for the work." Florence looked at everyone in turn until they agreed.

CHAPTER 14

ON SATURDAY MORNING, everyone woke at five except for Cherish, the youngest. *Mamm* allowed her to sleep in for no good reason, which had made the other girls grumble. Cherish's health had been fragile as a young child, but she had been fine for the past several years.

Florence had made everybody scrambled eggs and sausages for breakfast. It was important they have a hearty breakfast so they could have energy for their big day in the kitchen.

Mamm was the best pastry maker in their whole community, and as much as Florence tried, she could never match Wilma's skills. Wilma had said she was too heavy-handed, so the skill had passed over Florence and now Honor was the best out of the girls.

As Florence started on her morning coffee, she was entertained by watching her stepmother roll out the first batch of pastry. Skilfully and ever so lightly, she rolled out the dough with her old wooden rolling pin and then dusted her hands with flour and sprinkled some on the pastry. Then she rolled some more. When it was the right consistency and thickness, she lined one of several waiting pie dishes and sliced the leftovers with a sharp knife.

Honor was doing exactly the same as she worked side-by-side with *Mamm*, but it seemed she didn't have her mind on the job. "Why's Cherish asleep still? She should be working with the rest of us."

"She's younger than you," *Mamm* said. "There'll be plenty for her to do later. She won't be missing out. We've too much to do today to have any of you complaining or worrying about what others are doing. Just keep your mind on what you're doing."

"It's weird that you give her special treatment. I've noticed you've never even shown her how to roll out pastry."

Her mother looked at her in shock. "I have, Honor, I'm sure. Anyway, she was awake late last night not feeling well."

"Here I am."

Everyone looked up at Cherish, who was still in her nightgown.

"Sit down," Florence said. "I'll get you some breakfast."

Mamm told Honor. "When we finish up these ones, you can start on the taffy for the candied apples and Cherish can do the rest of these with me."

"Who's doing the stall today?"

137

"Joy and Hope."

They had already loaded the wagon with a table and their goods to travel to the usual spot three miles along where there was more passing traffic.

Florence wasn't very happy about Cherish being allowed to help with the pie pastry. Everybody loved their apple pies and came from far and wide. What if her sister didn't do a good job? She didn't seem to pay too much attention to anything she did. Where she cleaned in the house would always have to be cleaned again by someone else. She had the attitude that 'near enough was good enough,' but in Florence's book it wasn't. And *Mamm* never made Cherish redo her own poor-quality work.

"Watch her closely, *Mamm*," said Honor echoing the thoughts in Florence's mind.

A smile touched Cherish's lips. "It'll be fun. I've always wanted to have a go. I've

watched *Mamm* do it so much—that's why I
know it'll be easy for me."

FOUR HOURS LATER, the table and all the
counter tops were filled with baked apple pies.
Many years ago, *Dat* had installed two large
ovens into their large kitchen. They'd loaded
both of those ovens with pies, while Honor
used one of the stovetops for cooking up the
taffy. Favor had been given the task of inserting
a stick into each of the dozens of apples that
were soon to be dipped into the warm taffy.

Mercy walked into the room after pinning
out the washing. "I love the way the pies
smell when they're baking. This is what I'll
remember home smelling like."

Cherish had just sat down at the kitchen
table. "You mean this is the way you'll remember it when you marry Stephen?"

Before Mercy could comment, *Mamm* said, "I hope you'll make apple pies for Stephen when you marry, so your home will have this smell, too."

"Of course I will."

"And for all your *kinner.*" Cherish giggled.

Mercy joined in with her laughter unsure of whether Cherish was teasing her. It didn't matter. She would have many children with Stephen and she would bake them all pies.

Mamm said, "Mercy, you must remember to try to get him to move here rather than you move away."

Cherish butted in, "Why, just so you'll have more people to help in the orchard?"

"*Nee,* that's not what I was thinking! We'll miss you when you go, Mercy. I won't be able to bear it."

Joy and Hope walked into the kitchen just then, back from working the stall. Joy said, "We might all move away when we marry,

Mamm. Therefore shall a man leave his father and his mother, and shall cleave unto his wife."

"We don't need to keep being reminded what it says in the Bible. We have eyes and we can read for ourselves." Honor said. "Besides, that verse seems to say the husband should go where the wife is from."

"Stop it, girls. Can't we just have a nice day of baking without squabbles? Just one time?"

"It wasn't me," Joy said. "I was just talking about the word of God. What's wrong with that? Maybe if we all spent a little more time reading it, I wouldn't have to keep telling people what God's word says."

"I know and it's good that you read so much, it is. But sometimes it seems to be the only thing you say."

Honor lifted her chin. "*Jah,* people want to know what *you* think not what you think the Bible says."

Joy's mouth fell open in shock. "What I think is what the Bible says. Because—"

"That's enough. No one say another word." Florence said firmly, feeling a headache coming on. "Why are you both back so soon? Did you make so much money on the stall you thought you could come home?"

"There was no one around. I think it's a public holiday or something."

"Is it? I'm not sure. Wouldn't that mean more people would be about?"

"Believe me," Joy said, "I wouldn't lie."

"Everyone can have some free time now, when the taffy apples are finished," said *Mamm*." Then lunch, and then it'll be more pies."

"Can I make you a cup of tea, *Mamm?*" Florence asked.

"That would be nice, *denke*. I'll wait in the living room."

Florence set about making the tea and

put two cookies on a plate along with a frosted doughnut. Her mother always liked to have her tea with something sweet.

Once Florence had the girls organized with fixing lunch, Florence took the tea to her stepmother. *"Denke,* Florence. Sit with me a moment?"

Florence sat down next to her.

"She has to go where God leads her ..." She sipped on her hot tea.

Florence assumed Wilma was talking about Mercy.

Mamm continued, "but she might live a day's journey away and that means I'll hardly see her." Her mouth turned down slightly at the corners.

"That would be hard."

"I'd prefer her to live close by but who would she marry if she stayed here? There's really only the Johnson boy or one of the Storch brothers."

"There are many more choices than that."

Her mother opened her eyes wide and then blinked rapidly. "I know but she doesn't like any of them."

Florence officially gave up her protests about Mercy's intentions. No one was listening to her words of caution. It seemed as useless as Mercy trying to understand one of Stephen's jokes.

"What I am pleased about is she's not going on *rumspringa.*"

"I know she doesn't want to. We had a talk about it some months ago and she asked me why I never went."

"Possibly if you had, she would've felt she needed to. You've been a good example for my girls."

Florence smiled because she knew *Mamm* had meant it as a compliment, but it wasn't, not really. By saying it that way, she had made it clear she didn't see Florence as one of 'her girls.' "I'm glad I'm good for something."

Mamm chortled. "You're so good at everything, Florence. We could never do without you." She placed her teacup back onto the coffee table and picked up the frosted doughnut.

When her stepmother fell asleep, full of hot tea, cookies and doughnut, Florence slipped away to her room. There were no mirrors in the house, but she'd purchased her own small mirrored compact years ago. She opened the top drawer of her chest and pulled it out from beneath her underwear.

Then she took it over to the window, sat down and opened it. It had been a good while since the last time. What she saw was a shock. She did look years older, pale and weary with dark circles under her eyes. Since her father had died, she could never get enough sleep and that was evident in the fine feathery lines fanning their way out from the corners of her eyes. The bloom of her youth was fading already. The man God had for her would never see her youthful self, and that was sad. It wasn't how she wanted things to be. She'd come to terms with the fact that life was sometimes harsh, though, and things had rarely gone how she'd wished...

She shut the double-mirrored compact with a snap. It gave proof she was nowhere near as attractive as her half-sisters.

Her blue eyes, she'd been told were beautiful—some said they were the same shade as the sky on a bright summer's day. She'd gladly trade her shade of eyes for the symmetrical and pretty contours of her younger sisters' faces. Although she wasn't supposed to be concerned about her looks, she couldn't help it. She'd often thought that if God didn't want people to admire beauty, He wouldn't have given them eyes or a heart to appreciate what they saw. Why hadn't He made everyone look the same? Why were some born beautiful and others plain?

Her gaze was drawn back out the window. One thing would make her feel better and that was to walk among her trees. She got off the chair and hid her mirror back in the bottom of her drawer, and slipped out of the house before *Mamm* woke. Yes, there was a lot left to do today, but there was a lot every day. Sometimes, she just needed to be alone to feel better.

The fresh aroma of the trees wafting on the cool air revived her somewhat. *Gott* had blessed the orchard with good weather and good crops for the last few seasons. He'd smiled upon her family and in so doing had increased their savings. Florence gave Him thanks every morning for looking after them. Her father would've been pleased. In her mind, she saw *Dat's* smiling face. Happiness was to feel him near.

During her walk, she found her legs were taking her close to Carter's house. It was a good opportunity to look at the fence situation, she told herself.

Once she saw all was fine with his fencing reinforcement, and that the cows were on their side, she glanced over at the house hoping to catch sight of the intriguing and mysterious new neighbor. The white SUV that had been parked near the house was gone. Pushing him from her mind, she turned and walked back through the orchard.

Florence found it hard to relax because of all that still had to be done today. It would be easier if she wasn't in charge, but just as well she was or nothing would ever get done.

With tomorrow being their day of rest, they'd have to work late into the night tonight to get things ready for Monday. Still, many hands made light work and between her and *Mamm* and all of her sisters, they had many hands.

The baked goods would have to be taken out to the shop and placed into the huge commercial refrigerator, which was powered by an old generator. Before that though, she'd have to go out and start the often-finicky machine to get the refrigerator chilled down. A new generator was on the list of things they'd need to get before too long. *Before next season,* she told herself.

CHAPTER 15

THE NEXT MORNING, a weary Florence drove everyone to the Sunday meeting. She got down from the driver's seat and secured her horse.

When Florence looked up, the girls and Wilma were halfway to the house and no one had waited to walk with her. Feeling a little upset and very tired, she patted her horse, Chester, wishing she could've had the luxury of a sleep-in. Chester nuzzled his nose against her giving her sympathy. "You understand me, don't you, Chester? You would've waited for me if you were a person, wouldn't you?"

She left her horse and then noticed her heavily-pregnant friend, Liza, making her way toward her. "You haven't had the baby yet I see." Florence laughed sympathetically at the uncomfortable-looking way Liza was walking.

"*Nee,* but it can't be too far away. I hope. You'll be the first to know. Simon has instructions to call you first."

"I'm pleased to hear it."

Liza placed both hands over her belly. "Sometimes I feel I've been pregnant for years."

Florence giggled. "The *boppli* can't stay in there forever. It'll have to come out sooner or later." She noticed Liza's eyes were rimmed with redness. "Are you all right? You look like you've been crying."

"I'm just upset. We had another fight, last night."

"Not another argument?"

"Jah."

"Ach nee. A serious one?"

"We argued about what to call the *boppli.* I feel like I should give up and let him call the *boppli* whatever he wants, but it's my *boppli* too so I should have a say. I didn't give in and because of that it ended in a row."

"Did you tell Simon how you feel?"

"Nee because he'd blow up."

"You could put your favorite names into a hat and draw them out."

"We might have to. If he'll agree to that." As they strolled toward the house, Liza said, "I'm often sorry I'm not having a child with a man I'm truly in love with. Now I'm stuck with Simon. If only we were in love—really in love. It'd make all the difference."

Florence looked down at the pale gray compacted dirt that made up the driveway. She knew her friend needed somebody to talk with, but it was often a burden to hear such things. "You can only do your best," she mumbled.

"I know. I'm trying."

When they walked into the house, they found a spare bench on the women's side and sat down. When Florence saw Mercy was seated directly in front, she wondered if she should warn her once again not to enter into a hasty marriage. Anyone can get along on a couple of dates, but it took a whole lot more than that to make a marriage work.

Liza whispered, "I'm sorry I told you that just now, but I don't have anyone else to talk to."

"That's okay. I'm always here. That's what friends are for."

"And you'll never breathe a word to anyone?"

"Of course not. Never. You know me better than that."

Liza's lips curved into a smile, while Florence was more worried about Mercy.

When the meeting was over, Mercy walked outside hoping she'd get to talk with Stephen. But with so many people wanting to meet him and Jonathon, she knew she might only have time to say a few brief words to Stephen today.

She was working at the food table to assist the ladies when all of a sudden someone walked up to her. Looking up from handing out plates to people, she first thought it was Stephen and then saw it was Jonathon. And then, as though it had been planned to the second, they were suddenly alone.

He gave her a big smile. "Hello."

"Hello again." She looked around. "Where's Stephen?"

Jonathon sniggered. "You don't want to

worry about him. What you need is a man like me."

She stared at him wondering if he was joking. Stephen joked all the time so maybe Jonathon was the same. Just in case, she gave a little laugh.

"Come sit with me. Stephen said he'll be over in a minute."

"Did he?"

"That's right. Come on."

She looked at the other helpers and figured there were enough workers to allow her to slip away. She followed him to one of the empty tables that had been set up in the Fishers' yard and they sat down.

"What made you decide to come here?" she asked.

"I start a new job in another month, so it's a way for me to fill in my time and keep Stephen out of trouble."

Cherish suddenly sat down with them.

"Hello. I'm Cherish, and you must be Jonathon."

"This is just my youngest *schweschder,*" Mercy told him. "He isn't in any trouble, is he?"

Jonathon's face lit up when he looked at Cherish. "Hello."

Mercy bit her lip. The last thing she wanted was to marry a man who was in some kind of trouble. "Is he in any trouble?" Mercy repeated.

"Not yet, but there are all kinds of trouble he could get into especially if he's dating someone as pretty as you."

Cherish giggled and Mercy felt uncomfortable and looked around for Stephen. "There he is."

"*Jah,* he's talking to the bishop now, and he's telling Stephen to behave and be good."

"Has he been in trouble before?" Cherish asked joining in the conversation.

A smile beamed across Jonathon's face. "Could've been. I can't say."

"Jonathon, you must tell me if he's been in trouble before." Mercy rubbed at her throat feeling a nerve rash coming on. If something made her upset, her neck on one side would turn beet red.

The smile left his face and he frowned a little. "I was just having a little fun—joking."

She immediately relaxed and repositioned herself on the wooden bench.

"That's a problem she has. Mercy never knows when people are joking or not."

Jonathon smiled at Cherish, then he looked back at Mercy. "That's going to be hard for you. My family always jokes around with each other. That's what we do—how we relate to each other."

Mercy looked back at Stephen and was pleased he'd finished talking to the bishop. Their eyes locked and they smiled at one another and then he walked her way. "Here he comes now."

Jonathon placed his elbows on the table. "You really like him, don't you?"

"I do. I think he's very nice."

"Nice? Yes, that's how I described him, too—nice." He sniggered.

"Boring!" Cherish said.

Mercy wished Cherish would go away. She looked at Jonathon's face to see whether he was joking again, but he didn't seem like he was.

As soon as Stephen sat down with them, Jonathon said, "Who was that lady you were talking with before you spoke to the bishop?"

"No one. I can't think who it was."

"She was very attractive, but so are all the girls around here." He grinned.

Cherish giggled again, while Stephen leaned over to Mercy. "Ignore him. I wasn't talking with anyone. Has he been terrorizing you?"

"A little." She smiled knowing that was meant as a joke.

"That's rude. All I was doing was looking after her for you. Come with me, Stephen, and we'll get some food."

Both men stood, and Stephen said to Mercy, "We'll be back in a minute."

"I'll come with you," Cherish said half standing up.

"No! You stay with Mercy and mind our seats," Jonathon told her.

"We'll bring food back for you," Stephen said with a smile.

Mercy sat there and watched them walk to the food table, talking all the while, and she wondered what Jonathon was saying about her. She would have to develop a sense of humor the same as Stephen, but she wasn't quite sure how to do it.

"He's so handsome," Cherish said staring after them.

"I know."

Cherish scowled at Mercy. "Not Stephen. I'm talking about Jonathon."

"He looks all right, but you're far too young for Jonathon or anyone. He'd never take you seriously."

"He likes me already, I can tell."

After a few minutes, Stephen came back alone balancing three plates.

"Where's Jonathon?" Cherish asked once Stephen put a plate in front of her.

"He got distracted when he met some girls."

Mercy looked around and saw Jonathon sitting with two of the Yoder sisters.

"Excuse me," Cherish said taking hold of her plate.

Once Cherish left, Stephen smiled at Mercy. "I hope you'll stay for the singing. I'll drive you home if you're staying."

"I'd love that. We all stay for the singing normally."

"I'm looking forward to having you all to myself again."

She giggled and cut a portion of roast chicken and popped it into her mouth. All the while she knew Stephen was staring at her and she loved the attention. Then she noticed Cherish had sat down with Jonathon and the Yoder sisters.

CHAPTER 16

LATER IN THE DAY, Mercy felt sorry for Florence. Florence had wanted to stay on for the singing and *Mamm* had wanted to go home. Her older sister had no choice but to take *Mamm* home.

As she waved goodbye to Florence and her mother, Mercy realized just how much Florence did around the house and in the orchard. It wasn't always easy being the oldest. Florence had a lot of unpleasant stuff to do, along with the good, and she carried so much responsibility. She looked around for Stephen and couldn't see him.

Jonathon caught her eye and walked over. "Are you sure you won't change your mind?"

"Quite sure. I've already told Stephen he can take me home. But ..." He leaned closer with expectation dancing on his face, until she said, "My sisters need a ride home."

He stepped back and his face contorted into a grimace. "I've met Cherish. How many more of them are there?"

"Five. I mean, four more besides Cherish."

"Sure, I guess so. I'll take *Onkel* Samuel and Aunt Ada home and come back."

She smiled at his sad face. He would much prefer taking home a special young lady, that much was obvious. *"Denke,* Jonathon, I appreciate that. I'll tell them you're taking them home and I'll tell them who you are. I should've introduced you to *Mamm."*

"I met her. I told her who I was and I also met Florence."

"Ah good."

After Jonathon left her, she was walking over to her friends when Stephen walked up to her. "There you are. We were just talking about you. Joy was telling me a little more about you since you haven't told me very much about yourself."

She giggled. "I have too."

"You haven't. Not very much."

"I thought I did. We talked a lot on Saturday."

"There's talking and then there's talking. You don't talk very much. You didn't tell me much about yourself."

She put her hands behind her back. "What is it you'd like to know?"

"I'd like to know everything about you."

She gave a girlish giggle. "Everything?"

"Every single little thing. I want to know

everything you did today from the time you woke up."

"That's a little boring. I woke up and had breakfast and then came here."

"It might be boring to you but it's interesting to me. For instance, what was for breakfast?"

She smiled and was pleased how everything was going so well between them. She'd marry him right now if he asked her. "Granola. We make our own granola from rolled oats and other grains, and add nuts and dried fruits. It's really good, and it's filling."

"See? That's interesting, and it sounds really good. Tell me honestly, now. Jonathon wasn't giving you any trouble, was he?"

"*Nee.*"

"What was he saying to you?"

"Nothing. I asked him to drive my sisters home. *Mamm* and Florence left already."

He rubbed his chin. "That leaves you and me alone, truly alone?"

"That's right."

"My prayers have been answered. I can't wait to drive you home tonight."

"Me too."

At that moment, it was announced that the singing was just about to start.

"We'd better take our places," she said.

"I'll be counting every moment every word and every song until we can be back together."

She couldn't help smiling at his wonderfully romantic words. He was exactly what she wanted in a man. God had heard her prayers. She sat on the wooden bench between Joy and Honor and then the singing began.

From her back-row position, she could barely see Stephen. He was sitting in the second row from the front. Every now and again, when Jacob Hostetler moved his head just right, she caught a glimpse of Stephen.

Throughout the next hour, she noticed

between songs he turned around to catch a glimpse of her and she pretended not to notice he was looking at her.

After the singing was over, she gathered the girls together and told them, "Jonathon's taking you girls home."

"I wanna go with you and Stephen," Favor whined.

"Don't be stupid. You can't go with her, they want to be alone," Joy said.

It was rare that she and Joy agreed on anything.

"They spent all day Friday together. What could they possibly have left to talk about?" Favor grumbled.

"You'll know when you're older," Joy told her.

"I'll see you when you get home, Mercy," said Honor.

"Denke, Honor."

Honor and Joy shuffled the other three sisters off in Jonathon's direction and when they'd all introduced themselves, Mercy saw Jonathon's smiling face. She guessed he hadn't expected for all her sisters to be so attractive.

Before it was time to go home, though, there were the refreshments. While soda and cookies were being devoured by all, Mercy and Stephen decided to have an early start and they grabbed a few cookies and slipped away.

Once the buggy was out on the road, Mercy asked, "Did you enjoy the singing?"

"It was good. It's better than at home. There aren't enough good singers at home to sing loud enough to drown out the ones who can't sing."

She giggled.

"You find that funny but not my jokes?"

"I know what it's like when people can't sing and it can sound really off. Sometimes it even hurts my ears."

"That's how it sounds at home all the

time. None of 'em can hold a tune and I'm the same, I'm sorry to say. That's why I sing quietly and, just between you and me, sometimes I just mouth the words."

She laughed again pleased he'd said something she found funny. From the look on his face it made him happy too.

When they were on the dark lonely road under the moonlight, driving down the road and finally alone, he turned to her and said, "I honestly didn't think that my visit here would be anything like this."

"But your aunt told you about me."

"Do you really believe all the things she said about you? Someone like that would've surely been too good to be true, I told myself, but then here you are and you're real. You're *wunderbaar*."

She held her breath, waiting, just waiting for him to propose. Then there was silence. She finally broke it. "You are the first person to have said that—even my mother hasn't said something so nice about me."

"I can't see why."

"Me either," she said and they both shared a little laugh.

After twenty minutes of driving around, they decided it was time for Mercy to go home. As much as she was enjoying being close to him, she was disappointed he hadn't taken a perfectly good opportunity to propose.

She wanted to have a unique story to tell her *kinner* of how their *vadder* had proposed on the night of their first official buggy ride, but now she didn't have that. Her future story was ruined. Even though he'd said all those nice things to her, wasn't she good enough? What was he waiting for? "It looked like your *bruder* was enjoying himself tonight," she said only to fill the silence.

"He was happy because he was taking your sisters home."

"He didn't sound too pleased when I asked him."

"He can be grumpy sometimes. He says he's looking for a wife, so he'd be pleased with as much female companionship as he can get."

"My sisters are far too young to marry."

He glanced over at her. "Then how old are you?"

"I thought Ada would've told you?"

"No."

"I'm eighteen, and then my sisters are one year apart from each other. Honor is one year younger, then the next one's a year younger than her and so on. It goes like this, Me, Honor, Joy, Hope, Favor, and then Cherish—she's just turned thirteen. Then there's Florence, my older half-*schweschder* from *Dat's* first marriage, and I have two older half-*bruders*, Earl and Mark. You'll meet Mark, but Earl has moved away."

"I thought it was bad enough remembering the ages of my two brothers."

She smiled, but wondered if he was looking for a wife. Surely he was. He'd mentioned Jonathon was looking for a wife as though he himself wasn't.

When they arrived back at the Bakers' house, they saw Jonathon walking out of the door with Cherish giggling by his side.

"Looks like he had a good time."

"It does." She stepped out of the buggy and then Stephen got out and ran around the back of the buggy to meet her. "Thank you for a lovely time tonight, Mercy. Can I see you again real soon?"

His sincere question gladdened her heart. He did want to see her again. "Sure, any time."

"What about tomorrow?"

"Tomorrow? Isn't that too soon?" She tried to think what work Florence had lined up for her the next day and whether she was supposed to be at the roadside stall. "No, I'm sure that'll be all right. What about tomorrow afternoon? Wait, I forgot all about the harvest."

He laughed. "Me too. We'll be seeing each other early tomorrow, and every day." He took off his hat and ran a hand through his hair. "That's what I'm here for—the harvest."

She didn't want him to go. All she wanted was to put her head on his shoulder and for him to encircle her within his strong arms. Maybe he might give her a quick kiss or try to hold her hand.

"I'll see you tomorrow, Mercy."

"Okay."

He turned and got into his buggy and left even before Jonathon had gotten into his.

CHAPTER 17

WHEN SHE WALKED INSIDE, the girls were all lined up waiting to hear about her romantic date. How she wished she could tell them that he'd proposed. It would've been a dream come true. Instead, she had to tell them that nothing of the sort had happened.

The younger girls went to bed while *Mamm* went into the kitchen. Needing some parental advice, Mercy joined her mother.

"What am I going to do, *Mamm?* When

will he propose? I thought he'd do it on Friday and then I hoped he'd do it tonight."

"*Nee,* Mercy. He wouldn't be a responsible man to ask you that quickly. He has to get to know you first."

"What *Mamm* means is, he'd be a fool to marry you." Cherish giggled.

"I thought you'd gone to bed."

"I'm getting a drink of water. Why don't you marry Jonathon? *Nee,* he's probably too choosy."

"Stop it. Don't let her say things like that to me, *Mamm.*"

Mamm just stared at her and then Florence walked into the kitchen. "Just relax about it all, Mercy. It will happen if it's meant to happen."

Mercy gasped. "I can't help it. I'm not doing it deliberately. That's just how I feel."

Her mother held her head. "You lot will be the death of me. Now I have a dreadful headache and I'll have to go to bed. I can't take any of you any longer. It's just too much." *Mamm* walked out of the room.

"I always get the blame." Mercy pushed out her chair and ran away crying and reached the stairs before her mother. Florence walked to the door of the kitchen, and watched as Mercy took the stairs two at a time.

Cherish got herself a glass of water, took a mouthful and tipped the rest down the sink. Florence guessed she had just wanted to hear what her sister was going to talk about with their mother.

"*Gut nacht,* Cherish. Unless you want to help me clean up?"

Cherish pretended to yawn as she stretched her hands above her head. "Nah, I'm too tired." She walked out of the room.

It was then that Florence knew she'd be stuck with the washing up and the cleaning of the kitchen. At least it had only been the two of them for the Sunday dinner of leftovers. After a few minutes, Mercy was back and sat down at the kitchen table.

Florence wiped her hands on a hand towel and sat down beside her. The only reason she'd be back was to talk. "Don't be upset."

She looked up at her through misty eyes. "How can I not be? I need guidance from my *mudder* and she … says nothing."

"I know. Don't mind *Mamm*."

"Does he think I'm not good enough?"

"If he does, he has no taste at all."

"We get along so well. He's said so many lovely things to me and we talked about how we wanted our houses to be and everything."

"Are you in love with him?"

"I'm sure I am, but the only thing is he jokes all the time. I don't find it funny and I don't understand any of it. I'm not a joking person."

Florence didn't know what to say about that. Stephen did like telling his jokes.

"Maybe he jokes because he's nervous and thinks he has to fill in the silent moments with telling funny stories."

"*Jah,* that could be it. That must be it. *Denke,* Florence."

"Mind you, I'm not saying you should jump into marrying anyone without serious consideration and knowing him fully. The way I think about that is you must observe them over a period of time."

"You'll make a good *mudder* someday, Florence."

Florence smiled. "Maybe … someday."

CHAPTER 18

IT WAS the first day of their official apple harvest and they were up before daybreak. Even Cherish was awake. Florence's plan was to get all the orchard workers organized early, and then leave for her store at eight.

As they were finishing an early breakfast, three buggy loads of people pulled up outside the house. "Come on girls, let's go. You don't want to be late."

They greeted the usual families that came to help out on the first day of harvest. Today they'd have to abandon their roadside stall because it was 'all hands in the orchard.'

Wasting no time, everyone grabbed buckets and ladders and headed out to the orchard. Since there were no newcomers apart from Jonathon and Stephen, she let the others go on ahead while she gave the young men their instructions.

After she made sure all was going according to plan, she headed to her store. She opened the door and was pleased to see everything looked nice and everything was in its place. Forty-two pies were lined up ready, and taffy-apples in ranks by the dozen. It was the pies, she guessed, that would sell out first.

Just when she was congratulating herself that everything was running smoothly, she saw the signs propped against the wall. She was supposed to have gotten two of her sisters to put those signs out to direct people to the shop. That was how the locals knew the shop was now open and that was how the tourists found them.

Looking at the clock on the wall, she saw it was still early. Early enough for her to walk to put the signs out and make it back in enough time to open the shop. She took hold of the stakes attached to the two signs, grabbed the hammer and headed off. It was half a mile one way and half a mile the other.

Just when she was calculating whether she should go back and hitch the wagon, she heard a car. It was the white 4x4.

Carter slowed and opened his window. "Hello."

She seized the opportunity. "Could you do me a favor—if you're not in a hurry?"

"Sure, what is it?

"I have to put one of these signs up this way," she said as she gestured, "and one back that way. Would you mind driving me and my signs to do that?"

"Sure, jump in." He got out of the vehicle and put the signs and hammer in the back.

Once he was back inside, she clipped on her seat belt. "Thanks for doing this."

As he drove off he said, "You look a little flustered."

"It's just that my sisters usually do this and with everything being such a rush this morning, it being a Monday, and being our first day of harvest ... I completely forgot."

"You said your sisters usually did it."

"They do, but I forgot to remind them."

"I see. It's your first day of harvest? That's right, you told me it was Monday."

She directed him where to stop. He got out and insisted on hammering in the sign, and then he did the same in the other direction. When he got back into the car with her, she felt a little awful for having been so mean to him "I really appreciate you doing this."

"Sure, it's no problem."

"Where are you heading to today?"

"I'm just heading to town to get a few supplies."

She couldn't help smiling because he sounded like he was camping. And that's what he might've thought since he was a city-folk man and now he was living out in the country.

When he stopped the car at her shop, she said, "You've saved me so much time."

"Good, I'm glad."

"Stay here a minute." She went back inside and got two apple pies and took them out to the car. "Take these as a part of your supplies."

"No, I couldn't."

"Please take them."

"Can't I do a simple favor for you?"

"I'm grateful."

"At least let me pay you for them."

"I really appreciate your help."

"Thank you, Florence. Would you have

time after you finish here, to stop by and taste one of these with me?"

She was taken aback by the question and didn't want to be alone with him again. "We usually have a bit of a thing on the first night of harvest with the people who've helped. We make a big bonfire and cook over it. You're welcome to join us."

"Maybe I will."

She nodded. "Thanks again."

He smiled at her and then backed his car onto the road, and drove away.

SOON SHE HAD the first customers. A few hours later, she noticed her brother, Mark, and his wife, Christina, traveling up the driveway in their buggy.

They had helped with the harvest last year, but with them having just opened their saddlery store she'd thought they weren't coming. Apart from that, Christina didn't get along very well with anybody.

Going from the timetable Florence had written out, Honor came to take over at one in the afternoon to give her a break.

Florence was starving and was very much in need of a break. She walked into the kitchen and found *Mamm* making more apple pies. "I'm so pleased you're making more because we'll definitely need them for tomorrow."

"I thought you might."

And then she saw Cherish sitting down at the table staring into space. "Cherish, why aren't you out helping the others?"

"I didn't feel too good."

"Well I don't feel good most days, but it doesn't stop me doing anything."

"You're stronger than she is," *Mamm* said.

"I don't think that's true anymore. I just push myself and work through things when I'm not feeling well—like today and yesterday. I woke up with a headache and I started work and now I feel a little better."

Cherish scowled at her. "I do feel sick, Florence. And, I made everyone sandwiches just now and there was a mountain of them."

"Now you've upset her," *Mamm* frowned at Florence.

"That's good she made sandwiches. And if she's well enough to sit up, she could be peeling apples, or doing something to help."

"Why aren't you in the shop?" Cherish asked peevishly.

"I've been there all morning. I'm just having something to eat." Florence buried her annoyance and opened the gas-powered fridge and pulled out some leftover meatloaf from days ago. It smelled okay, so she made herself a sandwich. When she sat down in front of Cherish, she took a bite.

"You didn't make me one."

"I thought you would've eaten by now. Didn't you eat with the others?"

"*Nee,* I was too busy making them sandwiches. I haven't been doing nothing."

"Well, you could've made me one, too. Anyway, I've got to rush back to the store. Do you want to come with me and help?"

"You're mean. I'm going to bed so you'll believe I'm sick." Cherish stomped out of the room.

Mamm didn't say anything. She was too busy putting the top crusts on the apple pies. Then *Mamm* smiled, seemingly unaware of Cherish's recent outburst. "Did you see Mark and Christina are here?"

With a mouthful, Florence could only nod. When she swallowed, she said, "*Jah,* I saw them and I hope they stay for the bonfire tonight."

"They said they would."

"Good. We're going to have a *gut* season this year."

"It would be nice if your *vadder* could see

what a good job you're doing with the orchard, Florence."

Florence smiled. It was rare *Mamm* said something nice like that. "I couldn't do it without everybody's help. We all help each other and that's how we get things done, but that'll change in a few years as everyone gets married. Unless ... unless they marry local men and then their husbands can help in the orchard too at harvest time. *Jah,* that would be so *gut.*" Florence finished the last mouthful of her sandwich.

"There's no one for us to marry here."

Cherish was back.

Florence looked at her scowling face. "Well, you might change your mind about the boys you know when they turn into men. Time changes people a lot especially during those years."

"Yeah, well what are you going to do, *Mamm,* when we all move away. It'll be just you and Florence."

"*Denke*. I'll be here forever, will I?" Florence asked, feeling more on-the-shelf than ever.

"*Jah.*"

Mamm stopped decorating the edges of the pies and stared at Cherish. Instead of reprimanding Cherish for being rude, she simply whimpered, "I don't want any of you girls to move away."

Florence couldn't work it out. "*Mamm*, you do know where Stephen lives, *jah?* He lives in Connecticut. You won't see Mercy every day if they get married."

"Didn't you think about that?" Cherish asked her mother.

"Don't worry. They might not get married," Florence said trying to make Wilma feel better. "She might marry someone from around here."

Mamm placed her hands on her hips. "I don't know why you're against her marrying Stephen. Don't you want her to be happy?"

Florence dusted off her hands. "She's happy now." It seemed like whatever she said was the wrong thing so it was best to keep her mouth well shut and not say any more. She got up from the table, rinsed off her plate and left it in the sink. "I'm going back to the store."

"Aren't you going to wash your plate properly, dry it and put it away?" Cherish asked.

"You do it," Florence said. "Your tongue is well enough to talk, so put that energy into your hands."

Florence walked past her youngest half-sister and then slipped out of the house. All the while she could hear Cherish complaining about her. Florence didn't mind, she was pleased her stepmother had acknowledged all the hard work she did around the place.

THAT NIGHT, while the Baker family and their workers enjoyed the cookout, Florence kept looking around for Carter. She hadn't told Wilma or anybody else that he might be coming and she wondered how they would feel about an *Englischer* joining in with their celebrations.

She would simply do some fast talking and tell them he was their new neighbor. It was only right that they should meet him anyway since he was their closest neighbor.

The first few hours Florence spent hoping Carter wouldn't show and as the time slipped by, she found herself sitting on the edges of the group hoping he'd come.

Christina, her sister-in-law walked over to her and sat next to her. "You've been quiet all night, Florence. Why's that?"

"We've been very busy these last days and I'm a little tired. That might be why. *Denke* for coming. I know you're busy at your store these days."

"It's not my choice. We had to pay workers to cover for us so we could come here. I said to Mark that it didn't make sense for us to work for free here and then we have to pay our workers."

Florence didn't know what to say. *"Denke,* it was kind of you."

"It was kind of Mark. He's always looking after others."

"Why don't you and Mark come for dinner next week sometime? *Mamm* and the girls would love that. We don't see much of you these days."

"Why don't you all come to my place?" she asked.

"Denke, but it's so hard to get all the girls out of the *haus.* It'll be much easier if you and Mark can come here."

"It's easier for me if I stay where I am, too."

Florence smiled at her and wished she

could forever ignore her completely, but she couldn't. "The invitation is always there."

"And the same to you."

"You're welcome." Florence wasn't sure why she said you're welcome. From Christina's reaction, neither did she. She gave Florence a smile that was more of a grimace, stood, and then headed back to her husband.

Hopefully Earl will marry a girl I get along with.

Then she looked back in the direction of Carter's house. There was still no sign of him and people were standing up looking like they were about to leave. She still hadn't gotten around to each and every one of them to thank them, so she hurried to do just that.

CHAPTER 19

SEVERAL DAYS LATER, the harvest was nearly over. All the apples had been picked and sorted. Mercy had asked Florence if she and Stephen could make some apple cider alone, without any of her sisters interrupting. Florence had said that she'd do her best to keep them away.

The cider apples were in the shed and ready to be processed when Stephen and Mercy walked in.

"It smells nice in here, like perfume. It smells a little like cider already."

"These are mostly windfall apples, not the eating apples."

He nodded. "I know that. I helped sort them."

"Firstly, we have to wash them because most of them are covered with dirt."

He looked closer, *"Jah,* I can see that."

"After we wash them we grind them. Also, we make sure to pull out any rotten ones that we missed before."

"Don't get ahead of me. We wash 'em first, yeah? Then get out the rotten ones and then grind 'em."

"That's right. I'll show you."

They spread the apples into an old bathtub that they used for washing them, and blasted the apples with water. They threw the no-good ones into a bucket, and then put the others into the grinder and turned the handle. Out flowed the cider into the bucket below.

He laughed as he saw it come out. "Can we drink it now?"

"Sure." She lifted the heavy bucket and poured cider into a glass and gave it to him.

He blew off the froth and drank it. When he finished he had a froth mustache.

She held her stomach and laughed at him.

"This is so good. Hey, why are you laughing?"

"You have froth on your face." He scooped froth out of the bucket and tried to put it on her face. She squealed and ran away. "I'll stop chasing when you've got it on your face as well." He caught up with her and dabbed some on each cheek.

"Unfair," she said as she squealed with laughter.

Then he wiped it off for her with his fingertips, before he held her hand and led her back to the shed. "You drink some now."

"Okay."

He poured her some and she made sure she got rid of all the froth before she drank it.

When she stopped drinking, she looked at him. "There. How's that. Have I got any on me?"

He shook his head. "Not a bit. You've done this before."

"Once or twice. Come on. We have to make more and then we have to bottle it. Maybe tomorrow I'll show you how to make apple cider vinegar."

"Okay. As long as I can be with you, I don't care what we do."

"It's my job to make it. Everyone has their jobs to do around here. Florence has the place well-organized. She runs the orchard and the *haus*."

"What about your mother?"

She shook her head. "Not so much. Florence does most things around here."

As they made more cider, she explained

how to make apple cider vinegar, and then added, "Nothing goes to waste. We use the cores and the peels."

"I like the idea of nothing going to waste. How many apple trees do you have here exactly?"

"Hundreds. I can't tell you exactly."

"Can you guess what my favorite food is?"

She giggled. "What is it? Wait, let me guess. I think you would like roast chicken, and cooked ham while it's hot?"

He shook his head.

"Roast potatoes?"

He frowned and shook his head again.

"I give up."

"Apple fritters."

"I didn't know that. You would've enjoyed them the other night then."

"I did. I mentioned they were my favorite and I thought you would've remembered."

She smiled at him. "I thought you were just being polite."

"What's the food you like best?"

"The ones I just named. I hoped we'd like exactly the same."

"I do like all those things too. I like most food."

"You're easy to please."

"I know. I am very easy to please." He looked down at the apple cider that was flowing once again. "It's nice to learn new things."

"Now we have to bottle all this."

Once they were finished with the bottling process, they headed to the house carrying some of the bottles.

"I hope you're enjoying your stay," Mercy said.

"I am, and I knew I would."

She loved him saying nice things to her. "When did you know you would enjoy your stay here?"

"The day I saw you on the stairs. I knew you were the woman for me."

"Really?"

He nodded. "There's no doubt in my mind." He stood still and she stopped as well.

Their romantic moment was interrupted by her sister's dog running toward them at great speed. Now Mercy was annoyed. She wasn't annoyed at the dog; it wasn't his fault. Cherish wasn't far behind Caramel.

"You can't have him running at people like this, Cherish. You're going to have to train him."

"I will."

"Nah, he's fine," Stephen said as he put the bottles on the ground and bent down to pet the dog.

Cherish picked Caramel up. "I'm sorry. I had him tied up while I was watering the vegetables, but somehow, he got off."

"That's fine. I love dogs. This guy makes me miss Buster."

"You've got a dog?" Cherish asked.

"Yeah." He stood up. "He's my best friend. We've been through a lot together." He chuckled.

Cherish was smiling at Stephen a little too much so Mercy had to do something about that. "Take him back to the house. Can't you see we've got bottles?"

"I'm sorry, Mercy."

Cherish turned around and hurried away with her dog.

"She's a sweet girl."

"Sweet? You don't know her."

"Oh, really?"

"She's a bit of a troublemaker."

"I wouldn't have thought that, but I believe everything that comes out of your mouth. Mercy, I don't want to leave tonight to go back to my aunt's. I don't want to wait until tomorrow."

"It's not long."

They stood together talking not far from the house. "It's too long. Meet me tonight?"

"I can't go out at night. Florence would never allow it."

"I'm talking about me coming here without anyone knowing."

She gasped.

"Which window's yours?" He looked up at the house. "You said it was above the door but there are two virtually on either side of the door.

Pleased he remembered everything she said, she answered, "The one to the right. The other one is Florence's."

"Come with me." He walked over to the barn. "It'll be a full moon tonight so it'll be light. If I stand here, you'll be able to see me from your bedroom window. Then sneak out."

Should she do that? She'd get into dreadful trouble from Florence if she found out. She might even be grounded and not allowed to see Stephen ever again. When she stared into his green eyes, she found extra confidence. "What time?"

"I dunno. Late. Between midnight and two."

"What excuse will you give Samuel for taking the buggy? He'll want to know where you're going so late. It'll be a little weird."

"I'll walk."

"You can't do that. It's way too far.'

"It's not. I'll run to see you. I walk long distances at home and when I get bored walking, I run."

"Okay, but we'll get in the biggest trouble if anyone finds out."

"We'll just be talking. We never get enough time together and I'm due to go home soon. Please, Mercy. I love being with you."

She nodded. "Once everyone goes to

sleep, I'll be looking out my window. You will come, won't you? I don't want to wait up all night for nothing."

"I'll be here. I give you my word."

CHAPTER 20

WHILE FLORENCE WAS WALKING in the late afternoon, she wasn't thinking about her neighbor until she happened to be on that side of the orchard. She saw him walk out of his house. He looked up at her and waved, and when she waved back he started walking over to her. She headed to meet him and they both stopped when they reached the fence line.

"What are you doing?" he asked.

"Just walking. I try to do it every day."

"Don't you get enough exercise picking the apples to last you for a while?"

"I like to keep an eye on the trees and it's peaceful and I feel close to God."

He smiled and shook his head. "I know nothing about your God."

"He's everyone's God."

Raising his dark eyebrows, he said, "He's not if you don't believe."

She didn't want to get into a pointless argument, but she was convinced *Gott* believed in Carter.

"Got nothing to say?" he asked.

"Not today. I'd rather not." She looked up at the sky, then she noticed the cows. "Still got the cows I see."

"I do. I haven't eaten them yet. I'm thinking of becoming a vegetarian."

"Because of your pet cows?"

He gave a nod. "Maybe I'll just stop eating red meat."

That made her giggle.

"Anyway, I'm sorry I didn't make it over the other night when you invited me. I was nearly going, but I thought I'd be out of place."

She admired his honesty and it gave her a small insight into his character. "My family could've met you."

"I'll meet them soon enough. I still haven't been to get more of your food. Your pies were delicious."

"I'm pleased you liked them."

"I've got the new kitchen in already. I paid them overtime to get it in faster. Come and have a look."

"Not today." She stared at him and there was just something about him that appealed to her. It was as though he had some magnetic device attached to him and she was being pulled toward him. Yet, they were from two different worlds. Neither of them would fit into the other's. "I should keep going."

When she turned away, she knew she had

to stay away for good. It would be easy to spend time with him and get to know him better, but sometimes the easy things were the worst things to do.

CHAPTER 21

MERCY WAS SHOCKED when she looked out the window after everyone had gone to bed. Stephen was there already! She wasn't certain if Florence was asleep yet and, as usual, she'd been the last one of them to go to her bedroom.

She waved at him, unsure if he could see her, but he could because he waved back. Then she grabbed her shawl, tucked it under her arm, and slowly opened her door. Her heart beat hard as she slowly walked past

Florence's door to get to the stairs. The floor creaked a couple of times.

"Is that you, Mercy?"

"*Jah.* I'm just getting a glass of water. Do you want one too?"

"*Nee,* I'm fine. *Gut nacht.*"

"*Gut nacht.*"

She kept walking and hoped Florence wouldn't wait to hear her go back to her bedroom. Instead of going out the front door, she went out the back and then she hurried to meet him glad that the night was so bright. He saw her and came to meet her. Then he grabbed her hand and without saying a word pulled her into the barn.

Once they were in the barn, he closed the door and they both laughed.

"I can't believe you agreed to this," he said to Mercy.

"Me? I can't believe you asked ... and did you run?"

"I walked some and then I ran. Can we sit down somewhere in here?"

"*Jah,* we've got hay bales over here." In the darkness, they found their way to the hay and sat down. Then they ended up sitting on the dirt floor and leaning against the hay.

"I'm so happy you agreed to meet me."

"Me too. I want to spend more time with you too."

He put his arm around her and she sank her head against his shoulder. She closed her eyes and it felt right to be there with him even though she'd had to sneak out of the house.

"I'm pretty sure I'm falling in love with you, Mercy."

"I feel the same."

"I never want to leave your side."

She held her breath and thought she'd pass out. Was he going to propose? This was what she wanted and what she'd waited for. "I'd like that."

"I want to hold hands and walk in the moonlight, but someone might see us."

"Florence is still awake."

"Really?"

"Jah."

He breathed out heavily. "That's not good. You should go back. I don't want you to get into any trouble."

"But we've hardly had any time together."

"There'll be other nights. I'll come again tomorrow night and every single night after."

"Will you?"

"Jah."

"But it's so far for you to walk."

"It's worth it to spend more time with you. I'd walk that distance to spend one extra minute with you."

She giggled. "You would?"

"I surely would." He stood up and then pulled her to her feet. Once they were out of the barn, he took her into his arms and they hugged. She felt safe and protected wrapped in his strong arms. And then he stepped back. "You better go."

"Okay. I'll see you tomorrow, *jah?*"

"Of course. Your *mamm* and Florence are finding loads of work for Jonathon and me."

"Night, Stephen."

"I'll see you tomorrow. I'll be counting the minutes."

She hurried back to the house. Once she was in the kitchen, she filled up a glass with water and walked up the stairs. When she got to the top, Florence was standing there. "There you are. I didn't hear you come back to bed and I was just about to look for you."

"I had a snack too while I was there."

"You've not changed out of your clothes yet."

Mercy looked down at her dress and apron. *"Nee,* I was just about to now. I fell asleep in my clothes."

Florence seemed to believe her because she smiled and then put her arm around her and gave her a squeeze before she went back into her bedroom.

Mercy walked to her bedroom and looked out the window. Stephen was nowhere to be seen. She placed her water on the nightstand and changed into her nightdress before slipping between the covers. It was awful lying to Florence just now, but if she hadn't both Stephen and she would've been in big trouble.

CHAPTER 22

THREE MORE DAYS had passed and each night Stephen had met her in the barn. It was their secret time together. They talked of what they wanted for their futures, but still, he hadn't proposed and Mercy was deeply troubled. He'd said all the right things to let her know he was in love, but he wasn't saying the one thing she wanted to hear.

On Thursday when they were boxing the apples to take to the roadside stall, Stephen suddenly disappeared. She assumed he had just gone to the bathroom, but when she saw

Jonathon heading toward her instead of Stephen she wondered what was going on.

"Where's Stephen?"

"Wilma asked him to go to the markets for her."

"Oh, I would've gone with him. I can't imagine what she would've needed." They rarely went to the markets because they were fairly self-sufficient and what they lacked, they traded for with nearby farms.

"Will you come out somewhere with me on Saturday? We could do anything you want."

"*Nee.* I've already told Stephen I'd go out with him."

He dismissed the idea with a wave of his hand. "Yeah, but I'm sure you'd rather go out with me, wouldn't you?"

She didn't want to hurt his feelings but neither did she want to agree with him. It seemed he liked her, but the feelings weren't returned. "Sorry, Jonathon, but I like your *bruder.*"

"You're kidding, right?"

"*Jah,* I mean, no, I'm not kidding—we've grown very close. Extremely close."

He shook his head and scratched the back of his neck. "I can't figure out how he gets all the girls. He's got you and …"

Her heart froze. "And what? I mean, who?"

"Nothing."

"You must tell me. Does he have another girlfriend?"

"No, but he does have someone very interested in him. I thought they were close, but then he came here. They have the same sense of humor."

"Oh. I didn't know."

"Of course you wouldn't know. He's not going to tell you about the competition."

That was something she hadn't wanted to hear.

"Never fear. I can help you. I can help you if you want him."

She stared at him and everything clicked into place. That was why Stephen hadn't proposed and most likely that was why he was keen to spend so much time with her. He was deciding between her and another girl. "How can you help me?"

"For starters, he needs to know you've got a sense of humor. I notice you never laugh at his jokes. The other girl back home appreciates his jokes. He'd find you more suited if you joked a little with him."

She sighed. "I don't know any jokes. I only know the one's he's said."

"What I've got in mind is really funny. I'm not talking about telling a joke, I'm thinking that you should *play* a joke on him."

"Play a joke?"

He nodded.

"Okay. What do I do?"

He stepped closer and whispered, "It would be funny to tell him Buster died."

She stepped back. "His dog?"

Jonathon nodded.

"What are you two talking about?" In typical Cherish-fashion, she had appeared out of nowhere.

Jonathon smiled at her. "I'm just helping out two people in love. You go back into the barn and I'll come help you in a minute."

Cherish pouted. "I want to hear."

Jonathon shook his head. "Go now." He pointed at the barn, and Mercy was shocked when Cherish did what she was asked.

"Did you say to tell him his dog died?"

"That's right."

"That's cruel and horrible. Who would do such a thing? He's told me about Buster and he loves him."

"Ah, it would be horrible if it were true, but it won't be true. It'll be a joke. After you tell him about Buster's demise, tell him you were joking."

"Really?" She rubbed her forehead trying to figure out this joking stuff. None of it made sense. "I don't know."

"It's not a regular joke. It's called a practical joke and he'll be relieved that Buster's not really dead."

"I know he'd be relieved but I don't see how it's funny at all."

He frowned at her. "Has he asked you to marry him yet?"

That question got to her. He should've by now, and he hadn't mentioned the word 'marriage' in all the time they'd spent together. "Well … no."

"This might make the difference for you. He jokes around all the time and he'll feel happy he's found a woman who's the same."

"Do you think so?"

"I know so."

"Okay. Are you sure this is going to work?"

"Trust me. He'll think it's funny."

"I don't know if I can do it. He'll be upset if I tell him." She couldn't see it, but neither did she see any joke as funny and she so badly wanted Stephen to think she was the one for him. If he left and married that other girl, she didn't know how she'd cope. "Okay. I'll do it. Tell me exactly what to say."

After he went over exactly how to word the joke, they parted. Mercy went back to doing what she had been doing while waiting for Stephen's return.

Then she saw him coming back in the wagon with Florence. She waited until Florence was gone, and then she headed over to him. "Stephen. Hello."

He walked over to her, smiling until he saw her face. She was sick in the tummy for what she was about to say.

"Is all okay?" he asked.

She swallowed hard and told herself she had to do it. She had to be brave if she wanted to be Stephen's wife. "Everything is okay, but ..." She hesitated. If it was going to be funny about Buster, perhaps it would be funny and an even better joke if she substituted Buster. "Our phone in the barn rang just now. It was news for you from home."

He frowned. "Who would know to call here?"

"Someone called about your parents."

His eyes opened wide. "Are they okay?"

"I'm sorry to tell you this ... they're both dead."

CHAPTER 23

ALL COLOR DRAINED from Stephen's face on hearing the shocking news about the death of his parents. Grief and anguish caused him to throw himself on the ground. He wailed, writing around on the pebbled driveway. "No. It can't be." He looked up at her. "How? How did it happen?" Before she could answer, he pounded the ground with his fist.

He was taking it really bad and she knew she had to put an end to his heartbreak. "It's not true, Stephen. What I said just now was a joke. It's just a joke."

He stopped crying, sat up and wiped his eyes. "Are my parents dead?"

"*Nee.*"

"They're alive?"

"*Jah,* as far as I know."

He put his cut and bleeding hand over his mouth. "Why did you just say they died?"

She smiled and hoped he'd join her in a laugh. "It was just a joke."

He took a couple of deep breaths. "Who told you they died?"

"No one. I just made it up. It's a joke." When she saw him glaring at her, she knew it wasn't funny. Then it clicked in her mind that Jonathon had lied to her. "*Ach nee!* It was supposed to be funny. I thought you'd laugh." She crouched down on the ground with him and put her hand out to touch his hand, but he pulled it away.

"You'd thought it'd be funny to hear my folks were dead?"

"*Nee,* after that. When you found out it was all a joke."

"You refuse to help me collect the new generator just now and Florence had to come with me, and now this." He slowly picked himself off the ground, and dusted off his trousers. "You must hate me."

"Wait a minute."

He turned away from her and walked to his buggy.

"I didn't know you were going to get a generator. I heard you were going to the markets."

"It doesn't matter where, does it? Nothing matters now." He picked up his pace and she ran after him.

"Wait. Where are you going?"

"Home to Connecticut to see my parents. If they're still there."

In shock, she froze. She was losing him.

While he got his horse out of the yard and hitched it to his buggy, she begged him to listen to her. "Stephen, I'm so sorry. I thought it would be a funny joke. Don't go."

He said nothing the whole time and when he had finished buckling the last strap, he jumped into the buggy. "Goodbye, Mercy," he said, without even looking at her. The buggy started moving and she ran alongside it.

"I'm sorry, Stephen." He didn't answer and he didn't even look at her. "Can't we start this day over? I take it all back. I'm sorry." His gaze was fixed straight ahead. Then the horse broke into a trot and she could no longer keep up. "Will you be back tomorrow?" she called after him. There was no answer and then he was gone.

She turned to walk back up the driveway and saw Jonathon coming toward her. "He's gone, Jonathon. It didn't work."

Jonathon shook his head. "I saw it. I didn't think he'd take it like that."

"I didn't tell him Buster died."

He tilted his head to one side. "What joke did you tell him?"

"I told him his parents died."

His eyes opened wide and his mouth dropped open. It took a couple of moments before he spoke. "You what?"

"Told him your folks had died. I thought it would be funnier for some reason. If Buster dying was funny, I kind of thought it would be even more funny about his parents —hilarious even."

"Don't worry. It shows what kind of person he is to drive off like that. He's an un-reliable character. There's still work to do here and he couldn't care less."

"None of it was funny, was it, Jonathon? You lied to me."

"Hey, don't blame me. I didn't tell you to say what you said. What did you think he'd do? Now it's home time and I'll have to walk back to *Onkel* Samuel's." He shook his head and walked down the driveway. Then he turned and came running back. "Hey, forget him. He left you. I'll be back tomorrow." He gave her a big smile, then he turned and walked down the driveway.

Mercy stood there in shock, trying to take everything in.

What had just happened?

"Wait, Jonathon." Cherish ran past Mercy to catch up with him.

Tears stung in the back of Mercy's eyes and she ran all the way to the house.

She flung the back door open and Florence stood there in front of her. "What's upset you?"

"Oh Florence. It was terrible and too embarrassing to tell anybody what I did. I can't even believe it. I'm in a bad dream. A horribly bad dream and one I can't wake up from."

Florence gasped and took hold of her by the arm. "Sit down, Mercy."

She took a deep breath and sat down at the kitchen table, while Florence pushed some freshly ironed clothing to one side.

"It can't be that bad." Florence wore a sympathetic smile as she sat beside her.

"I told Stephen his parents died."

Florence's jaw dropped. "How?"

"*Nee* they didn't!"

"I don't understand. They're not dead?"

Mercy shook her head.

"Why would you tell him they died when they didn't?"

Mercy told Florence the whole story of what Jonathon had suggested she do. "I don't know why I thought it would be funnier to tell him … what I told him. I can't even say the words now."

"Where's Jonathon now?"

"Walking home. Well, walking back to Ada and Samuel's place."

"Apologize to Stephen and tell him truthfully what happened."

"I can't. I mean, I think I did. He'll never talk to me again."

"He'll calm down."

"When he does, he'll be all the way back in Connecticut. He'll never look at me the same again."

"It's all life experience. You can learn a lesson."

Mercy sobbed on Florence's shoulder and Florence put her arms around her and let her cry. Mercy didn't want to learn a lesson if it meant losing the man she loved.

Florence said, "Don't listen to others when your heart and your head are telling you something else."

"It wouldn't have been funny about the dog either. Right? Why would Jonathon do that, Florence? He must've known Stephen wouldn't think it was funny."

"I don't know. The only reason could be if he likes you and he was trying to split you and Stephen apart."

"I thought that too, but that's horrible if he did that. It's an awful thing to do."

"You should tell Stephen the truth. You were trying to impress him and Jonathon told you to tell him his dog had died and then—"

"I can't. I can't tell him something like that about Jonathon. Then he'll be mad at Jonathon too."

"You can't go too badly wrong with the truth." Florence handed her a handkerchief that sat atop the ironed clothes.

"Denke." Mercy blew her nose. *"Mamm* said you don't tell the truth when it is going to hurt someone's feelings."

"Jah, but if you think you could marry this man, it might be a slightly different thing. He's not just anybody."

"Oh, Florence, why is everything so hard? Will love always be so elusive for me?"

Florence couldn't help laughing. "You're young and you've got some years ahead of you before you start complaining about love."

"Some people don't care about being married, but I wanted to be a young *mudder*. I want to have ten *kinner* by the time I'm thirty."

"Don't give up on Stephen just yet."

Mercy wiped her eyes. "Do you still think there's a chance?"

"There's always hope. Pray, and then leave it in *Gott's* hands and let Him sort it out, okay?"

"I guess I have to. There's really no other choice."

"No other good choice, anyway."

"What will I say if *Mamm* asks why he left so early? I don't know what to say. She'll ask questions when he doesn't arrive tomorrow."

"Say you had a little disagreement."

"Will you tell her for me?"

"Of course." Florence gave her another

hug. "Will you be okay now? I've got some things to take care of."

"I'll be fine."

FLORENCE WALKED out of the house and hitched the buggy. The only thing she had on her mind was talking with Jonathon and telling him exactly what she thought of him.

Then she'd tell him that the right thing to do would be to tell his brother exactly what he'd done. If Jonathon confessed then Mercy wouldn't have to be the one to tell Stephen what happened.

Florence found him about a mile from the house and the worst thing of all was that Cherish was walking with him. She pulled the buggy over to the side of the road a little way in front of them. She got down and walked back to them. "Cherish, turn around and go home."

"Why? I'm just having a walk. You go for a walk every day, so why can't I?"

"Do as she says, Cherish," Jonathon said softly.

"When will I see you again?"

He rubbed the side of his face and looked over at Florence. "It's hard to say. Soon I hope. Go on. You don't want to get into trouble."

"I'm going." Cherish turned and walked back slowly, dragging her feet.

Florence turned her attention to Jonathon. What she felt like doing was slapping him hard, but she managed to control herself. It was no surprise he didn't look too happy. "Can I have a talk with you for a moment, Jonathon?"

He hunched his shoulders. "Look, I know what you're goin' to say. You think it was all my fault."

"And wasn't it?"

"Wait. What are we talking about here?"

"We're talking about how you talked Mercy into telling that dreadful joke. Only it was no joke."

He took off his hat and ruffled his dark hair in an agitated manner. "I didn't say to tell him that our folks had died."

"I know exactly what you said. She told me. It was bad advice from the beginning, and you knew it was going to drive a wedge between her and Stephen."

"I guess so." Jonathon put his hat back on his head.

"You admit it?"

"Yeah. It's not fair. All the girls like him." He looked back at Cherish and at that moment, she'd turned to look at him and she waved. His hand raised a little, and then he turned back to face Florence.

"Do the right thing, Jonathon. You have to tell Stephen what you've done. Tell him what you said to Mercy and leave him to straighten this whole thing out."

"I can't do that."

"You can and you will. Otherwise, I'll tell him myself. Also, everyone will learn of it. What about your folks?"

He took a step closer and stared into her eyes. "You wouldn't."

She stepped even closer until there were only two inches between them. "You might think you know me and the kind of person I am, but you know *nothing*. I'll tell everyone and I'd enjoy the telling."

He took a step back. "It'd make Mercy look stupid."

She took a step forward. "I'm not bothered by that. She did listen to you so …"

He rolled his eyes and took another step back "Okay. I'll tell him."

"Good. And do it right now, just as soon as you get back to Ada's, so he has a chance to straighten things out with Mercy. She likes him a lot. You could be standing in the way of them having a life together."

"He'll hate me forever, but if that's what you want."

"I can't control his reaction and you have to take accountability for what you've done. Just be sure to tell him. All of it, too. Exactly what was said and how it happened. It's better for all concerned if you make this confession on your own." Florence walked back to the buggy feeling good that she'd been able to help. Then she hurried back to him. "Get in the buggy. I'm taking you to Ada's right now so you can tell Stephen sooner. I'll let you out near the *haus* so no one sees me."

Reluctantly, he agreed.

FLORENCE HAD DRIVEN SLOWLY to Ada's place lecturing Jonathon all the way there. She was convinced by what he said that he would confess all. When she got back home, she was unhitching the buggy and deliberating whether or not to tell Mercy about her talk with Jonathon, when Cherish ran over to her. She thought Cherish was going to ask her about Jonathon and she, in turn, was going to tell her to keep away from him because she was making a fool of herself.

"Someone needs you!" Cherish said.

"What? Is everything all right?" From the look on Cherish's face, she wondered if someone had started a fire in the kitchen by burning something, or if someone had burned themselves or been otherwise injured.

"It's Liza; she's had the *boppli* and she's asking for you."

"Is she okay?"

"Yeah, she just said she wants to see you. Well, she didn't. Simon called here and I was near the barn and I answered the phone and that's what he told me to tell you."

She buckled up the side pieces of the harness she'd just undone. "I don't know what time I'll be back, but can you make sure there's dinner for everyone and a meal set aside for me?"

"Sure."

"That would be *wunderbaar, denke.*"

On the way there, she wondered what her friend would've wanted to see her about. Liza had her sister and her sister-in-law both there as birth helpers and Ruth, the midwife, lived less than a mile away. She half thought Liza would've wanted her at the birth as well since they were the best of friends, but Liza had never asked.

Liza's house was five miles away so the trip didn't take very long, but it felt halfway to forever because she was so eager to get there.

After she finally arrived, she secured her horse, and Simon, Liza's husband, came out to meet her with a grin that reached from ear to ear. "We have a *boppli.*"

"So I heard. I'm so happy for you."

He walked up to her and hugged her. The

man had normally acted gruff and standoff-ish, and it was so out of character for him to act this friendly or excited. In the back of her mind, Florence hoped it would be a lasting change.

"How's Liza?"

"They're both good. C'mon inside—I'll take you up to her. She's been asking for you."

"I can't wait to see her and the *boppli*."

"He's big they tell me. He's just shy of ten pounds."

"That is big."

"Can you wash your hands first? Do you mind?"

"*Jah,* of course. I wouldn't dream of being near the *boppli* with dirty hands."

He took her coat and over-bonnet and she walked into the washroom. When her hands had been scrubbed, they walked up the stairs and she found Liza alone in the bedroom. Simon left her there and went back downstairs. The new mother's eyes were glued to the baby she cradled in her arms.

A weary-looking Liza turned to look at her with a smile. *"Denke* for coming. I've sent my birth-helpers and the midwife into the kitchen to get me something to eat. I've worked up a good appetite. I wanted to talk to you alone."

Florence edged closer, feeling a little nervous about getting her first peek at the baby. "Give me a good look at him." She saw he was sleeping. "He looks a little like Simon. He's not wrinkled at all like other new *bopplis.*"

"I know. Ruth said he looks as though he's a few weeks old already. I can't believe that he's here and I made him."

Florence giggled. "Not just *you* made him."

Liza joined in with her laughter. "Simon might have helped a little."

"I can honestly say I don't think I've ever

seen Simon so happy. He's like a new person."

"That's what I want to talk to you about. Forget all those things I said about him. He's been so good through the birth and I think … I know it was just me complaining about him for no good reason. Probably because I was feeling a little frustrated and letting myself be dissatisfied with life. Now that's all changed. I've got a purpose now. Simon and I can share our love with this little one."

"I can understand that. Don't worry, I would never ever have said anything to anyone anyway."

"But I don't want you to even think anything bad about him."

"*Nee,* I won't." She swiped a hand through the air. "All bad thoughts are gone, just like that."

"*Denke.* I want you to be one of the first to hold him."

Florence leaned down, lifted the baby and

cradled him in her arms, carefully minding his neck. He opened his eyes, and she was sure he looked right at her before going back to sleep. "My, he is a *big* little *bu!* What have you called him?"

"Malachi, after Simon's *vadder.*"

"That's a nice strong name." Florence guessed Simon had won the name battle, or Liza had relented to save the peace. "He's so precious. I hope to have my own one day."

"Of course you will. It'll happen. You just have to be patient."

Florence smiled at her friend. It was such an easy thing to say for someone who already had a family of her own to love and to care for.

She smiled again and then kissed the baby's bald head. He smelled so good. "His skin is so soft. Don't worry I washed my hands. That's the first thing Simon asked me to do."

"He's going to be a *gut vadder.*"

"I'm pleased. I didn't even know you were in labor."

"Things happened pretty fast. My helpers were only here for an hour or so before he arrived. Oh, how was your harvest?"

"Really good. We had so many helpers this year, and loads of great apples, and the shop's been quite busy."

"That's just your side business isn't it? The shop, I mean. You make most of the money selling apples?"

"True, but the earnings from the shop and the roadside stall help a lot."

Liza yawned.

"You must be tired."

"I feel okay, not too bad for birthing such a big baby, and I'll recover."

Staring at Liza she wondered how painful childbirth was. "I'm so happy for you. I feel as though something good has happened for me too."

"Of course. You're his Aunt Florence."

"I like the sound of that. It's my first time to be an aunt."

"How's Mercy doing with that new boy?"

Florence pulled a face. "Long story—I'll save it for another day. Can I do anything for you? Get you anything?"

"*Nee,* they're bringing me up some soup."

She passed the baby back. "I'll go now, but I'll visit you again soon. Is that okay?"

"Always! Please do."

She left Liza's house amazed at how relationships could change. Perhaps if two people who were once so at odds could reunite, then there was hope for Mercy and Stephen.

Simon and Liza's house, once full of arguments, was now filled with peace and love.

On her drive home, she drove past Carter's house and found herself smiling at his 'pet' cows grazing in the fields.

CHAPTER 24

MERCY HAD STAYED AWAKE all night praying. After breakfast, she was washing up the dishes when she saw Stephen's buggy coming to the house. She asked Honor to finish the dishes for her while she hurried out to meet him.

She waited until he pulled up and then walked over to meet him. Judging from his smiling face, she knew he was ready to forgive her. "Stephen, you're back."

He got out of the buggy. "I never left to go back home."

"I'm so sorry."

"It's okay. I'll just let the horse into the yard and then we can talk." When he'd done that, he turned to face her and then said, "I know what happened. Jonathon told me everything."

"It was a horrible thing to do. I wanted you to think I was funny and for some twisted reason I thought it would be funny and you'd like me more."

He chuckled. "You've got a *funny* way of showing your feelings. I know my brother's part in it. He also told me he said I liked some other girl, but I don't. Why didn't you tell me all that yesterday?"

She shook her head. "I didn't want to tell you what he said. He's your *bruder*. I didn't want to cause bad feeling between the two of you."

"I understand, and that makes me like you all the more."

She studied his face. "Can things be back to normal?"

"Yeah. All is forgiven. Let's forget it ever happened."

She put her hand over her heart. "I'm so relieved. I don't think I'll forget it, though, or the lesson I've learned."

He wagged his finger at her. "Just never do it again."

"I won't. I'll never do anything like that again."

"Good. Now, what has your *Mamm* lined up for us to do today?"

"I don't know, but she said you could stay for dinner tonight if you want and then she said you could help me with the goodie bags for the school kids after dinner." As they walked, she explained, "We've got a group of children coming tomorrow to see how the orchard works and what we grow, and what we produce. We give each of them a bag with goodies in it to take home."

"That's a nice idea. I'd love to help."

She smiled at him.

"Does your mother know about what happened yesterday afternoon?" he asked.

"*Nee.* She has no idea. I guess I would've had to tell her if you didn't come today. I'm glad you came back. Is Jonathon coming today?"

"I'd rather not talk about him for a while."

"That suits me just fine." She stared at him and wondered what their children would look like. With his green eyes and her bluish-green ones, they'd have to have green eyes for sure—at least some of them. Their hair would be light and maybe tinged with gold, and maybe darken as teenagers to match her reddish-brown. It was fun to imagine.

AFTER A BUSY DAY of delivering apples to three different markets, Stephen stayed on and had dinner with the Baker family. He got along well with everyone and Mercy knew all her sisters liked him, even Florence. After the dishes were done, Stephen and Mercy were left alone in the kitchen to prepare the bags for tomorrow's visitors.

"You like children a lot, don't you?" Stephen asked her.

"Of course I do. I like them very much."

"Me too. I could tell. Would you like to have your own soon?"

"I really would." She smiled at the thought as she tied a bow on another one of the bags.

"That would mean you'd have to get married."

She looked up at him, pleased they were talking about marriage. "Of course. I wouldn't have children without being married."

He laughed. "I didn't think that you would."

"I'll get married, and then have children."

After he looked around, he spoke again. "Would you consider …" He gulped. "Would you consider marrying me?"

She looked into his eyes. This was the moment she'd dreamed of. "For real?"

"Yeah, for real."

"You want me to marry you?"

"Yeah, I wouldn't ask if I didn't want it to happen."

"I will marry you, Stephen Wilkes."

He smiled. "I like how you said my full name."

"And I like everything about you. You'll make a *gut vadder* and a *gut* husband."

"You'll make a *gut fraa*." He stood and held out his hands. She stood up and put her hands in his.

She stared up into his eyes and then his

head slowly moved closer and he stared at her lips. She closed her eyes ready for her very first kiss. Before their lips met, she heard a squeal. They jumped apart and she looked over to see Cherish in the doorway of the kitchen. "What is it, Cherish?"

"*Mamm* wants to see you."

"Right now?"

"*Jah,* right now."

"Can Stephen come too?"

"I guess."

Cherish disappeared, and then Mercy looked at Stephen, but the moment was gone.

"We better see what she wants," Stephen said.

"It better be important," she said under her breath as she headed out of the kitchen.

Stephen followed her and they found *Mamm* in the living room working on her cross stitch sampler. She was only awake this late because of their visitor. The other girls had gone to bed. Even Florence, who normally stayed up late. She had been working so hard lately she'd told them she was too tired to push through it tonight.

"What is it that can't wait, *Mamm?*"

Mamm looked up at her. "What do you mean?"

"You wanted to see me."

She shook her head. *"Nee."*

"Cherish said you want to see me about something."

"I don't think so."

Why did she constantly allow people to trick her? If Stephen hadn't been there she'd have found Cherish and told her exactly what she thought of her.

"Shall we tell her our news now?" he whispered.

"Okay with me, but do you think we should?"

He nodded and then they both looked at *Mamm* who was staring at them.

"What's going on?"

"Stephen has asked me to marry him."

Mamm squealed, tossed her sampler into the air and ran to hug Mercy. She paused, pushed her out to arm's-length and looked her in the eyes. "You did say, 'Yes,' didn't you?"

Mercy laughed as she answered, "Of course, *Mamm*."

Mamm chuckled and folded Mercy into a warm hug. Then she hugged Stephen. "This is the best news I've had in my life. I'll be a *grossmammi* soon."

Stephen raised his eyebrows. "Not too soon, Mrs. Baker."

"When do you plan on getting married?" *Mamm* asked.

They stared at each other, both waiting for the other to speak. Finally, Mercy said,

"We don't know. This has only just happened."

"You'll have to get married here rather than Connecticut because it's a little difficult for all of us to travel all that way."

"I was already thinking of getting married here," Stephen said. "I'm sure my folks won't mind."

"This is so good. Am I the first one to find out?"

"*Jah.*" Mercy giggled.

"You must call your folks and tell them right now, Stephen."

"What? Now?"

"*Jah,* now. It's still plenty early. Go and call them from the phone in the barn. I won't tell the girls until you tell your parents, Stephen. They should be the very next people you tell. It's only fair."

He rubbed the back of his neck. "I guess so. I hadn't really thought about it."

"I can wait. I'll keep it quiet until you tell them."

"Come with me, Mercy. I'll put you on the phone so you can say hello."

Mercy giggled nervously. "Okay." This wasn't how she'd expected to meet her future in-laws.

CHAPTER 25

MERCY HAD to keep her secret overnight and into the next morning, as Stephen's parents hadn't answered their phone.

Eventually, at midday they answered their phone. They sounded a little hesitant about the news and not nearly as joyful as *Mamm*. It put a bit of a damper on Mercy's excitement, but Stephen assured her it was just that they were surprised. He told her they'd soon be happy for him and eager to meet her.

The next thing Stephen and Mercy did was find her sisters and tell each one.

The last people to tell in Mercy's family were her half-sister and her two older half-brothers. Mercy and Stephen kept an eye on the shop and when the last customer of the day left, they headed to share the news with Florence.

WHEN FLORENCE LOOKED up from tallying the day's sales and saw both Stephen and Mercy approaching the doorway wearing grins, she knew they had happy news.

"Guess what? We're getting married," Mercy blurted out as soon as she walked into the shop.

Florence pushed the last of her doubts aside. She had as much chance at stopping the wedding as stopping a runaway buggy. Besides, she didn't want to. She'd gotten to know Stephen a little better when she'd traveled with him to fetch that new generator, and she thought he'd showed wisdom and maturity by forgiving Mercy so wholeheartedly. "I'm so pleased for both of you." She gave them each a hug.

"Are you sure, Florence?"

Florence laughed. "Of course I'm sure. I'm really happy for you."

"*Mamm* wants us to get married here at the *haus* and we want to get married really soon."

"Oh?"

"I'm calling my folks tomorrow and we'll arrange a time. And then we'll have to see if that time's all right with your bishop."

"You haven't told him yet?" Florence asked.

The young couple stared at one another.

"*Nee*. We should go there now, Stephen."

"I guess so. I've never done this before." He rubbed the back of his neck.

All three of them laughed at that, and

Florence said, "Best head over there right now and tell him."

When they hurried out of the shop, Florence knew the Bakers were in for a busy time preparing for a wedding. It would take place right here at the house. Although she was pleased everything had worked so well for Mercy, she was a little saddened. She was still alone in spite of being years older than Mercy. Where was her man?

MERCY GAVE Stephen directions to Bishop Paul's house.

"Will he tell us we haven't known each other long enough?" Stephen wondered.

"*Nee.* I don't think so."

"I hope not. I don't want to have to convince him. I just want to arrange a date when we can get married."

"A Friday. A Friday before Christmas

would be what would suit me. Early December."

He screwed up his nose. "That's over a month away."

She giggled, pleased he wanted to marry her quickly. "There's a lot of preparation that goes into a wedding. There's the food and the clothes and people have to know a long way ahead so they can plan to come."

"I guess."

"And it's our special day and I want everything to be perfect."

"It will be."

When they arrived at the bishop's house, he was just getting into his buggy. Bishop Paul stepped down when he saw them. They got out too, and met him halfway.

He smiled at them and his long gray beard moved upward on his face and then he adjusted his thick black glasses. Stephen said, "Are you heading off somewhere, Bishop Paul?"

"It's nothing that can't wait. I have to collect Hannah from her friend's *haus,* but she won't mind staying a little longer. I was early anyway." He then eyed them carefully. "Have you come to see me?"

"*Jah.*"

The bishop smiled again, as though he knew why they'd come. "Come into the *haus* and we can sit. But you'd best secure your horse first."

Once they were sitting on the couch in the bishop's living room, Mercy felt her throat constrict. At that moment, it all became real and she realized the enormity of the decision they were about to make official.

"We want to marry," Stephen began.

"Okay ... and you've both had a good long think and you've talked about whether it's right? You haven't been here long, Stephen."

"I know my own mind and we're both of age."

"That's right." He rubbed his beard.

"From the looks on both your faces I'd guess you want to marry without too much delay?"

"First Friday in December," Mercy blurted out, fighting against her light-headedness. Stephen suited her perfectly and there was no doubt in her mind.

The bishop calmly rose from his chair and picked up a large black book that had been on a wooden chair by the fireplace. He also picked up a pen that had been underneath the book. When he sat down again, he said, "This is my wedding appointment book. First Friday in December is the fifth. And it's available."

"Perfect," Mercy said.

Stephen gulped and Mercy could see how nervous he was. "Can we marry on the fifth, then?"

"I don't see anything that would stand in your way. Your parents are all in agreement?"

"*Jah*, both are," Mercy said.

"Let's write you in for that date." The

bishop asked for their full names and birth dates, and then told them what else needed to be done. Including, he reminded them, that they'd both need to be baptized into the Amish faith prior to marriage, which is something they'd clean forgotten. They also made a date with him for that.

Minutes later, they drove away from Bishop Paul's, elated. "It was so easy," Stephen said.

"I knew it would be. There was no need to be so nervous."

"I just didn't want anything to go wrong."

She took hold of his hand pulling it away from the reins. "Nothing will. Meet me tonight outside the *haus* at midnight?

"Sure."

"We can talk more about our future."

He squeezed her hand tighter.

THAT NIGHT FLORENCE had stayed up late sewing. When she found herself nodding off, she folded up her sewing and crept up the stairs. As she did so, she met Mercy tiptoeing down the stairs. Mercy jumped when she saw her. "I thought you'd be asleep," Florence said, looking her up and down. Mercy was still in her day clothes.

"*Nee,* I'm just getting a glass of water."

"You drink an awful lot of water at night. Perhaps you should drink more throughout the day?"

"Sure. I'll give that a try. *Gut nacht.*"

"*Gut nacht,* Mercy."

MERCY POURED herself a glass of water so she wouldn't be lying to Florence—not so much, anyway, and then hurried out to meet Stephen. She'd seen him from her window and he was waiting in the usual spot.

CHAPTER 26

IT WAS FRIDAY, December 5, and Florence
Baker sat in her living room along with a
crowd of people, waiting for Mercy to marry
Stephen Wilkes.

Sitting beside her was her stepmother,
who bumped Florence's shoulder, and then
leaned in and whispered, "I don't know why I
encouraged this wedding."

"It's too late for regrets."

"I know."

Florence was the only one who'd been
against Mercy marrying a man she barely

knew, but Florence was more confident now she'd gotten to know Stephen a little better. "They're perfectly suited. Don't you think so?"

Mamm sniffled and dabbed at the corners of her eyes with a white handkerchief.

With little sympathy to offer, Florence faced the front. If anyone should be crying it was she—watching her six-years-younger half-sister get married before her. However ... to get married she needed a man, and there was no one in whom she was remotely interested.

From her back-row position, she cast her gaze over the crowd, looking at the single men. It was a futile scan; none were her age. Then there were the older widowers, all of whom had seen their better days—and they all sported long graying beards. Not the kind of man she saw herself with.

Even if *Gott* placed the perfect man in front of her, he'd have to be pretty open-minded. She couldn't leave her beloved apple orchard. Her situation was hopeless, but she'd always have her apple trees.

After two hymns, a reading and a long talk given by Bishop Paul, Mercy and Stephen were pronounced married. When everyone rushed to congratulate them, Florence stayed in her seat worrying about her remaining five half-sisters. What if Mercy marrying young had set a trend her sisters thought they should follow?

It wouldn't do to have them all rushing into marriage.

They were all easily led except for Joy and she was a different case altogether. Joy was an abrupt and no-nonsense kind of person, who took after their maiden-aunt, Dagmar. Florence expected the same outcome for Joy.

Florence then looked over at her friend Liza, two rows in front, happily holding her sleeping baby. Now that Liza had a child, she insisted her marriage was happy. Florence hoped that it was so, and suspected Liza regretted confiding in her over the years. The things Liza had said made Florence think twice about marriage. Well, they would've done so if she'd ever even come close to it.

Reminding herself there was work to be done, Florence rose to her feet and headed to the kitchen to take charge of serving the food. *Mamm* had left her to arrange the food for the roughly three hundred and fifty guests that were expected. The number of people coming to a wedding was always an unknown, as no invitations were sent. Word went out that there was to be a wedding and people would travel for miles to attend. There were always hundreds of guests.

As well as planning the menu, ordering the food, and arranging for the women to cook, Florence had also sewed the wedding clothes for the bride and groom and all their attendants. In all, that was three dresses, capes, aprons, and *kapps,* and three suits for the men. The men all had their own black bowties and shirts, so it was a saving that she didn't have to sew those. Because of the extra workload of Mercy's wedding as well as running the apple orchard, Florence had hardly been out of the house for several weeks.

Back in the kitchen as they put the food into serving dishes to be taken out to the tables, squeals rang out as *Mamm* and her best friend, Ada, had only just realized that since Stephen was Ada's nephew, *Mamm* and she were now relatives of a sort.

Once most of the work was done, Florence said to *Mamm,* "Why don't you sit down outside and enjoy the wedding? I've got enough helpers in here." To seat everyone, an annex had been set up in the yard with tables, and there was a special bride and groom's table at the front. Large gas heaters either side kept the guests warm.

"Are you sure? You always work so hard."

"Go on. It's Mercy's wedding. Celebrate with her."

"*Denke,* Florence." *Mamm* hurried out and Florence looked out the kitchen window to see *Mamm* sitting down next to Earl at the closest table to Mercy's. Earl was Florence's older brother who'd moved to Ohio.

This was the first time he'd been back in over two years. He'd left not long after their father had died. She made a mental note to speak with him as soon as she could. He'd arranged to stay with a friend rather than at the family home, so she'd best use this opportunity. She missed him, but he never got on too well with *Mamm,* which was the reason he'd moved away.

The groom's parents and his younger brother couldn't make it to the wedding, but they'd sent their apologies by letter and added that they were eagerly awaiting the newly married couple, excited to welcome them into their home. Of course, Jonathon, the trouble-making older brother was in attendance today.

She looked at Jonathon and then noticed her youngest half-sister walk over to him. She'd told Cherish many a time to keep away from him. It was staggering to Florence that Jonathon and Stephen were so different. They were similar in looks but poles apart in personality. She was keeping a close eye on Jonathon.

What is Cherish up to?

Florence found someone to take over her job in the kitchen and moved closer to Cherish and Jonathon to hear what they were saying.

"I happen to know you've been invited to Honor's birthday dinner next week."

"That's right." Jonathon smiled at her and then looked around. "I'm looking forward to it. Seems funny my younger *bruder* has married your older *schweschder*."

Cherish pouted. "That's hardly fair that

they got married and we have to wait."

He laughed. "It's just how things have turned out. That wouldn't have been a problem if you were the second oldest *dochder* instead of the youngest."

"It's my fault? Hey, wait. What do you mean second oldest?"

He chuckled. "By that I mean I like Honor. She's the second oldest if you don't count Florence."

"You're not serious, are you? She's deadly boring."

"I'm deadly serious and she's not boring. Not to me anyway. She could be to you."

"I—"

Having heard enough, Florence walked over to them. "There you are, Cherish. I've been looking for you to help in the kitchen. We all have to take a turn."

"I will soon." She looked up into Jonathon's eyes and said, "I'm talking to Jonathon right now."

Annoyed by her dismissiveness, Florence stepped forward and took hold of Cherish's arm. "Jonathon, would you mind if I steal her away from you?"

"That's fine."

Florence steered Cherish across the yard.

"Don't you know it's rude to interrupt?" Cherish said trying to free herself from Florence's grasp.

"I heard what you were saying and I saved you from making an idiot out of yourself. Remember, you're only thirteen." Then they were in the kitchen and Florence told one of the ladies to give Cherish a job. She was given the job of scraping food off the plates and stacking them for washing.

Once Florence was satisfied Cherish wasn't going to talk her way out of the kitchen, she put the irritation of Cherish out of her mind and helped herself to a plate of creamed chicken with broccoli. She walked outside and sat down with Liza and her husband, Simon. Liza was busy jiggling her baby up and down to stop him whimpering.

Florence ate a quick mouthful and looked around to see Jonathon now talking with Honor. They seemed engaged in a serious conversation. This wasn't good.

When baby Malachi opened his mouth and yelled, Liza's husband got up and cheerfully took him from Liza to walk him around.

Florence leaned over and whispered to Liza, "What could Jonathon possibly have in common with Honor? She's so lovely and quiet and he's a bit of a schemer. I know for a fact that he likes her."

"How do you know?"

"I just overheard him saying it."

Liza looked where Florence was staring. "Are they dating?"

"Not that I know of." Florence nibbled on the end of a fingernail. "I don't like it."

"Relax. I don't think she's interested in him."

"I hope you're right." Florence blew out a deep breath and then looked around for her stepmother. She was talking and laughing with Levi Brunner as though she didn't have a care in the world. Everything always fell on Florence's shoulders.

"Why are you so worried? I had loads of crushes on all kinds of unsuitable men when I was her age or thereabouts."

"I don't trust him. He concocted a plan to break Mercy and Stephen up because he wanted Mercy for himself. At least I think that was his reason. Either that or he just wanted to be mean to his *bruder*."

"Why didn't you tell me?"

"I don't know. I think Malachi was only just born—the very day, now that I think about it, and I didn't want to tell you any worrisome things."

"You should tell me these things." Liza looked back over at Jonathon and Honor. "It's hard to say. They're only talking."

"*Jah,* at the exclusion of everyone else and they've been like that for several minutes."

"Should you say something?"

"Like what?" Florence asked, no longer interested in the food.

"Just go over there and talk to them."

"I guess I should."

Florence picked up her glass of soda and headed over to them. When she was halfway there, Jonathon whispered something to Honor and by the time she reached them he was gone. She faced a glum-looking Honor.

Honor frowned at her. "Why did he leave when he saw you coming?"

"You'd have to ask Jonathon that. I don't see what you have in common with him. He's so much older."

"I like him."

Florence's heart sank. "*Jah,* well just remember your age."

"Age means nothing."

"It does. You're a child, technically, and

he's a man. I'm going to tell him to keep away from you." She turned to walk away and Honor reached out and took ahold of her arm nearly spilling her soda. Florence looked down at the strong grip Honor had on her. She'd never realized she was so strong.

"Don't say anything. Please, Florence."

Florence took hold of her soda with her other hand and then pulled her arm away. "I'll say anything I please. What do you think *Dat* would say about you liking Jonathon?"

"He'd be pleased I found someone."

"Found someone? You've got years ahead of you to think about that. Worry about that when you reach my age."

"I won't be as old as you and still living at home. I'll have my own family way before then."

She looked into her sister's radiant and youthful face. Didn't she know life wasn't so simple? In life, there were struggles and pain, not to mention disappointments. She didn't want any of her sisters to regret choosing a man in a giddy moment to then face a life of hardship when she found him unsuited to her. There was no divorce—no way out. Marriage was binding and final.

"Nothing to say?" Honor asked lifting her chin slightly.

"I don't want to be still living at home either, but there's worse out there." She stared into her sister's blue-green eyes and it struck her that her own life was so pitiful that Honor was looking to escape the same fate. Suddenly, her sisters finding someone by the time they were eighteen didn't seem so young. "You'll find someone when you're older. When you're Mercy's age, and until then I won't have you even thinking about boys. Well, boys, but not men and ... and not men like Jonathon Wilkes."

Honor lifted her chin again and folded her arms across her chest. "I like him and I'm only one year younger than Mercy. Honestly, you can't stop me from seeing him. You're not my *mudder*."

None of the girls had talked to Florence like that before and that was worrisome. She was losing control and she wondered what her father would've done. She summoned all her strength and took a step closer. "You'll do what you're told. Once you're older you can do as you please. I'm going to talk with Jonathon right now to tell him to stay away from you."

"You wouldn't."

"Watch me." She turned away and found Jonathon at one of the food tables heaping food onto a plate. "Jonathon, we need to talk."

He looked around at her. "Sure. What is it?"

"It's Honor."

"What about her? She's the *schweschder* next oldest after Mercy, right?"

"*Jah,* the one you've spent the last half hour talking with."

"I thought so. There are a lot of you. Anyway, what about her?"

He was making this very difficult. "Stay away from her."

He drew his dark eyebrows together and his face contorted into confusion. "Why?"

"She has a childish crush on you and … well, it'd be better for her if you stayed away."

"Sure. Does that mean no more dinner invites?"

Florence nodded. "Until she gets over it."

"No problems. I'll keep away." He chuckled. "Are you sure she has a crush?"

It sickened her to her stomach that he found it amusing. "It's not funny."

"It's kind of flattering."

"Not really. She's only turning seventeen in a few days." She was pleased she got that in, and she also noticed he swallowed hard.

"I'll do as you say. I have no interest in her, I can assure you of that. Just so you know."

Florence laughed. "Of course you wouldn't, not at her age. I didn't think you did, but it'd be best for all concerned if you keep your distance."

"Okay sure. I can do that."

"*Denke.*" Unconvinced, Florence headed back to Liza and sat down.

"You're brave. I saw you talking to him. What did you say?"

"I told him how old she was."

"He would've known."

"He should've, but I drove the point home and asked him to stay away."

Liza looked over at Wilma. "Your *mudder* didn't even notice."

"She wouldn't. She lives in her own little bubble coasting over the surface of life." Florence poured herself a soda from the jug and took a mouthful. It was hard being the disciplinarian in the family.

"In other words, she has no backbone," Liza said.

"*Nee,* it's not that so much. She can't cope with anything. She was far harder on the girls when *Dat* was alive."

"She might've taken his death harder than she lets on."

"*Jah,* maybe. Now she's upset Mercy will be gone for a year."

"Are Mercy and Stephen staying at your place tonight?"

"*Nee.* They're staying at Ada and Samuel's house and then they're leaving in the morning. We'll all miss her." She looked over at the happy couple. "I haven't even congratulated them yet. I'll do that now."

On the way to congratulate the newly-married-couple, she saw Earl sitting alone. She took the opportunity to talk with him.

He smiled when he saw her walking toward him.

"How are you?" she said when she'd sat next to him.

He pulled her into a one-armed hug. "Pretty much the same. I had thought I'd be coming back here for your wedding, not Mercy's."

She rolled her eyes. "Don't *you* start. *Nee,* there's no one who suits. What about you?"

"There are a couple of ladies, who might be contenders."

She giggled. *"Gut.* I'm happy to hear it. You must write to me more."

He nodded. "I will. I've missed you."

"And I've missed you dreadfully." They stared at each other for a moment, both missing their father and neither wanting to mention him. Earl would also be missing their mother. He'd have memories of her, and Florence was sure that was why he'd never gotten over their father marrying again.

"I should congratulate our *schweschder* and our new *bruder*-in-law."

"I'll be leaving tomorrow," Earl said.

"*Nee*. Can't you stay awhile longer?"

"I need to get back for work. It was all I could do to take a couple of days."

She sighed and nodded. "Well, don't you dare leave without saying goodbye."

"I'll find you and say goodbye tonight because I leave first thing, early tomorrow morning."

Florence nodded.

CHAPTER 27

IN THE EARLY hours of the next morning, all the girls and *Mamm* crammed themselves into one buggy to travel to Ada and Samuel's to say goodbye to Mercy and Stephen. It was most likely the last time they'd see them for a year, until they moved back.

When the horse and buggy traveled up Ada and Samuel's driveway, they saw the taxi. *Mamm* started weeping at the sight. Stephen was helping the driver put their luggage in the trunk while Mercy was on the porch saying goodbye to Ada and Samuel.

Then Mercy ran to the buggy. "You're late. You nearly missed us."

"You know what it's like to get all of us anywhere on time," Florence said as she stepped down from the buggy.

The girls got to Mercy first and then *Mamm* got out of the buggy and Mercy wrapped her arms around her. "I'm going to miss you so much."

"We'll all miss you too."

Florence threw the reins over the post and joined in with the farewells.

"Bye, Florence," Mercy hugged her. *"Denke* for everything. I know it was hard work sewing all those clothes, but you did them just right."

"Jah, well I wasn't game to make a mistake."

Mercy smiled. "I know I haven't been the easiest person to live with leading up to the wedding, but I'll make it up to everyone when I get back home."

"Have *bopplis* soon," Cherish called out.

"*Jah,* we want to be aunts, don't we, Cherish," Favor said with a giggle.

"*Jah.*"

"Hush, girls," *Mamm* said, frowning.

Then Stephen walked up beside Mercy and said goodbye to everyone in turn. Ada and Samuel stepped off the porch and stood with the Baker family and watched Mercy and Stephen get into the taxi.

Stephen and Mercy waved to them all as the taxi slowly drove away.

Mamm burst into tears. "She's gone."

Ada put her arm around her. "Why don't you stay here—if Florence can fetch you later?"

Mamm looked at Florence through tear-filled eyes and Florence nodded. "Sure, I'll do that."

After Florence's half-sisters said goodbye to their mother, they all got back into the buggy.

WHEN THEY CAME BACK HOME, Florence told Hope and Joy to unhitch the buggy and tend to the horse. "Then you can all have a couple of hours off," Florence announced.

"Yay, free time," squealed Honor.

"*Jah,* but then there's the cleaning up to do. The only ones who'll get out of that are the two who are going to the markets today."

"It's Hope and me," Joy said. "We'll take the buggy and go now, if that's okay."

"No stock to take with you?"

"*Nee.*"

"Okay. Take the buggy."

Three girls headed into the house, two got back into the buggy, and Florence finally had a tiny bit of freedom. There was no more wedding sewing and no more wedding organization.

Normally, she loved to sew, but sewing to

a deadline—and in such quantity—was too much pressure.

Adding to that, Mercy wasn't the easiest person to sew for. She'd had exact ideas how she wanted everything to be and mostly told Florence about it after she'd done it differently. There had been hours of picking out stitches, but thankfully the younger girls had done that job.

It was finally time for Florence to think about herself for a moment and take that walk for which she'd been longing. It was one of the few things that calmed her. The other was a hot bath, but it was rare that she could linger in a tub without one of her sisters banging on the door saying they needed to use the bathroom.

She'd been longing for this stroll through the orchard—her sanctuary. She'd only been walking twice in the last several weeks and both times she'd noticed her mysterious *Englisch* neighbor, Carter Braithwaite, hadn't been home and his house had seemed closed up. Had he decided country life wasn't for him and he'd headed back to the city?

Walking along the orchard with the apple trees either side of her, she was away from all annoyances. She walked on and on allowing the icy wind to blow her worries away while the weak winter sun moved higher into the sky.

When she was near the southern fence-line, she heard whistling and her heart rate increased. That had to mean Carter was there, but she couldn't see him anywhere. The whistling got a little louder and then she saw him walking around from the side of his house. She couldn't resist walking closer. When he looked up and saw her, he stopped whistling. His hand shot up in the air and he smiled and waved. Then he jogged over and they met at the fence.

She felt different when she saw him this time. Her life could've been made easier if he'd been born an Amish man, but had that been so, he'd probably have been married by now—to someone else.

"I haven't seen you for a few weeks." She wished she could've taken that back. Now he knew she noticed he'd been gone.

"I had to leave for a while and take care of something."

Take care of what exactly? she wondered. That reminded her that she still didn't know what he did for a living. The *Englisch* world was a bit of a mystery, but she was certain no one would pay him to play chess against his computer. By his own admission, he wasn't even a good player. That was the only thing he'd told her about himself apart from the fact he was overseeing house renovations and he was from the city.

A big smile covered his face. "I've got my new bathroom and kitchen installed. Would you like to see them?"

"Some other time, thanks. I've got so much to do back at the house."

"I thought you could rest up now that your harvest's over."

With that comment, his appeal lessened. It irritated her when people thought that having an orchard was a breeze. It was hard work and the work didn't stop just because the harvest had finished. "Is that what you think? You think we just have apple trees and only work a few weeks of the year?"

"No." He shook his head. "I know that's not right. You have the stall that your sisters run down by the main road. I've seen them there—driven past. I even bought some pickles from them once."

"We work all year around in the orchard. The girls just do the roadside stall for extra income. The orchard is hard work the entire year, throughout all the seasons."

"I'm sorry. I didn't know." He shifted his weight from one foot to the other. "What do you do at this time of year? There's no fruit on the trees, so ..."

"We all still work in the kitchen, canning and making preserves. As for the trees, we prune them and check regularly for any health issues."

His gaze traveled to the orchard behind her. "The trees look dead to me."

She frowned and then remembered he was from the city, so she kept things simple for him and launched into the spiel she gave the school children on their yearly tours. "They aren't dead. They're still working hard." *Never resting, much like myself,* she thought. "They're gathering nutrients from the soil to be ready for the next growing season. You see, they lose their leaves so they don't have to waste the nu-trients on the leaves. They store everything through the colder weather, and the colder it is, the better the apples the tree produces."

"They need the cold. I see, well that makes sense."

"Good." Could he have been married and he was recovering from a divorce? Maybe his wife died in a tragic accident. He folded his arms over his chest and she found herself looking at his left hand for a wedding ring or a sign that one had been there. There was nothing.

"You're certainly passionate about your trees. It seems like they're your life."

"Every orchard owner's the same. Taking care of trees is time consuming and some-times all consuming."

He scratched his neck. "Seems so. Were you having some kind of an event yesterday at your house?"

"Yes. My sister's wedding."

"One of the bonnet sisters got married?"

"Please don't call us that. Or … or I'll call you the … the hatless man with no siblings."

His lips twitched. "Hmm. That would be

quite a mouthful. I'm surprised that *you* didn't get married. Aren't you the oldest?"

She didn't need to be reminded. "I am, but there's no law that says the oldest has to marry first."

"No, but I thought your family was traditional, and I would've thought they'd want the oldest to marry first. And then each one down the line."

"Not at all. You're wrong."

He grinned. "It's possible. I thought I was wrong once before ... but I was mistaken."

She frowned at the cheekiness of his grin. They stared at one another and there was some kind of moment between them; she was sure he felt the same. "I have to go."

He stepped forward nearly stabbing his chest on the high barbed wire that ran on the top of the fence between them. "Will you be walking again tomorrow?"

"I try to walk every day, but sometimes I don't get the chance."

"I'll keep an eye out for you." He beamed her a smile. "Just in case."

She gave him a little nod, then turned and headed back to the safety of her trees.

He wasn't going to see her tomorrow or any other day. She had to keep away from him and, somehow, she had to stop thinking about him.

As she walked on, she wondered about the differences between the Amish and the *Englisch.* Then she thought about her community and all the different personalities of everyone she knew. There was Jonathon who'd tricked Mercy into unknowingly doing something unkind. Thankfully, Stephen forgave her and they were reunited. Then there was Wilma, who lived off in the clouds somewhere leaving Florence to step in and do her job of keeping the girls in line. Then there were all the differing personalities of her half-sisters.

Why aren't people more like apple trees? she

muttered. She stopped and put her arms around the trunk of one of her trees, resting her head on a low branch. It was the unpredictability of people that made them disagreeable and difficult. With apple trees, you always knew what you were going to get. They fruited in the summer and fall, dropped their leaves in the winter, and then came to life again in the spring.

Florence wanted to keep walking and be with her trees, but in her heart, she knew the girls wouldn't start cleaning until she got home. She'd have to further encourage them by saying it would be a surprise for their mother if the place was spotless on her return.

CHAPTER 28

THAT AFTERNOON, Florence went back to Ada's and collected a happier Wilma. They arrived home and all the girls fussed over *Mamm* and made sure she was comfortable as she sat working on her sampler while Florence reheated wedding leftovers for dinner.

When they all sat down to eat, Florence saw *Mamm* staring at Mercy's empty chair and considered removing it, but that might've made *Mamm* even sadder.

Once they said their silent prayers of thanks for their food, Honor said, "When can

I marry? Seventeen? I don't have to wait until I'm eighteen, do I?"

"*Nee*, with permission, but you won't be marrying Jonathon because he's so much older and unsuited."

Honor frowned at Florence while Cherish was too busy playing tug-o-war with the chicken wishbone with Favor to notice Florence had mentioned her unlikely crush, Jonathon.

"How do you know Jonathon's the one I like?" Honor asked. "I could be talking about Isaac, Christina's *bruder*. He's moved in with Mark and Christina you know."

Mamm tipped her head to one side. "Then, who were you talking about? Jonathon, did you say? Or Isaac?"

Cherish interrupted, "Did someone say Jonathon?"

"*Nee*," Florence snapped. "Who do you like, Honor?"

"Christina's *bruder,* Isaac, I'd reckon," Cherish said. "He would suit you perfectly."

"Oh him. I met him at Christina and Mark's wedding too," *Mamm* said. "He's nice. But isn't Jonathon staying with Mark and Christina?" *Mamm* asked. "That's what I heard from Mark's own mouth."

Florence added, "It'll be awfully crowded in their tiny place."

"Nee, Mamm. Not exactly. Jonathon is staying in their barn. It's got living quarters there. Isaac is staying in their actual *haus,"* Honor said.

"And when can I marry?" Cherish asked. "How old do I have to be?"

"A lot, lot older than you are now. That is for certain," Florence said.

"I was asking *Mamm,* not you." Cherish looked over at *Mamm.*

"Florence is right. You're still too young for such talk."

Cherish pulled a face. "You two always stick together."

Honor stared at Cherish and said, "What is unfair is that you're continually talking about boys when you're too young to even go on a buggy ride."

"We need a rest from weddings for the moment and any talk of weddings," *Mamm* said.

"Jonathon likes me and I like him. Our love will find a way. I love him more than you do, Honor," Cherish said.

Florence stared at Cherish. "Love?" That was exactly what Florence had feared. "I don't think he takes anything seriously, Cherish. Perhaps he's the kind of man who loves everyone? That's what I think, so just be mindful of that."

"*Nee,* he's not. He stayed with me the whole day yesterday and there were lots of other girls there."

Florence sighed knowing that if Jonathon

had been talking with Cherish it was only to get closer to Honor.

"Jonathon likes me not you," Honor told Cherish. "I'm not meaning to be rude or nasty, but you're far too young for him to even think about liking you."

Cherish's face screwed up as though she was going to cry. "You are being mean."

"Excuse me. I'm no longer hungry." Florence headed out of the kitchen leaving her dinner and leaving *Mamm* to cope with the girls. She could be the disciplinarian for once. There were problems ahead with both Honor and Cherish liking Jonathon and she couldn't think of someone worse for one of her half-sisters to like.

With the background chatter of the girls, Florence sat down at the desk in the corner of the living room. In need of more lighting, she lit the lamp that stood atop the desk and then pulled the financial ledgers out of the drawer.

Florence sighed. Keeping the books was a burden she wished was someone else's, but there was no one good with numbers like she was. Without even referring to the books, she knew they were doing okay financially, but if they had one bad season they'd be in trouble.

They'd made a lot of money in the last few months, but that had to last for the entire year. With the colder weather, she'd told the girls to stop the roadside stall until the weather was more favorable. She didn't want them freezing to death on the side of the road. The income from the daily stall was sorely missed.

"What's wrong?"

Florence turned to see Honor beside her. "Ah, just looking at how we're doing."

"We're doing okay, aren't we?"

"We always get by. I'd like to have more to put away. You're too young to remember, but we had three bad seasons in a row and had to sell some of our land. And we had to sell it for less than it was really worth. There weren't any buyers around. Anyway, *Dat* selling the land to the Graingers got us out of trouble and then we were okay after that. The next season was good and we've been okay ever since."

"I wondered why he sold off that land and those buildings."

"Buildings? There's only a cottage and the barn."

"There's the smaller house too at the back of the property. I saw it once. I haven't noticed it lately. Maybe it got pulled down or fell over in a storm."

"I vaguely remember that now. Was it made from stone?"

"I'm not sure. So, you'd like enough in the bank in case something bad happens?"

"*Jah.* That new generator set us back. There's always something going wrong or something that needs fixing."

"I guess the wedding cost a lot too."

Florence grimaced. The food for the wedding and the fabric for the clothes had added up to a small fortune. "I didn't want to say, because I'm really happy for Mercy and Stephen, but *jah*."

"We really should keep selling anything we can to keep the money rolling in. I'll probably get married in a year or two."

"I know." Florence nodded, not wanting to face that until it was upon her. "It's no use thinking of the roadside stall. There are so few buyers around right now, so it's not just the possibility of you girls freezing to death."

"We'll hope and pray that nothing goes wrong with the weather and all that."

"That's best, but *Gott* gave us a brain to use and I believe He wants us to be practical and do all we can."

"How about I get you a hot cup of tea while you look at those books?"

Florence relaxed her shoulders. "That

would be nice. It's just what I feel like. I had to get out of the kitchen though." She whispered. "I couldn't listen to Cherish one moment longer. And … Jonathon of all people. I'm sorry, but you know I don't like him. Not one little bit because of the prank he pulled on his *bruder* and Mercy."

"I heard about it and he's truly sorry. He just made one mistake. *Gott* says to forgive."

Florence chuckled. "That might take me some time. I can forgive him, but that doesn't mean I want him anywhere near you."

"You'll get used to him. When you get to know him better you'll like him. I'll bring you a cup of hot tea."

"*Denke,* Honor." Florence knew Honor had been won over by Jonathon's charming personality. He knew all the right things to say to win her heart and that was a worrisome thing. At the same time, Florence knew there was most likely very little she could do about the situation and what's more, if she forbade her to see him that would make her want him all the more.

Florence was delighted when Honor brought the remainder of her dinner out to her along with a cup of hot tea.

CHAPTER 29

WHEN THE GIRLS had all gone to bed, Florence sat with Wilma in the living room. They were in their nightgowns and ready for bed, but they both decided they'd stay up for a little while. Wilma worked on her cross stitch sampler and Florence crocheted squares for a blanket.

"I can't believe Mercy is all grown up and married. Even more unbelievable that she chose him before she met him. It was as though God had whispered in her ear and told her Stephen was the one. I can tell you I was worried. She was so determined to marry him before she'd met him. That could've gone horribly wrong for her."

"I know what you mean." Wilma said smiling, most likely thinking of the grandchildren she'd have.

While Florence was pondering love, she wondered how much of it was determined by *Gott* and how much of it was the choices that He allowed people to make. She'd previously thought the ones who'd rushed into things were the ones with unhappy marriages.

Maybe she was wrong about that theory.

There was so much she'd asked *Gott*, but He still hadn't answered.

Why did some women find their husbands young while others had to wait?

Some, like her *Dat's* older *schweschder* Aunt Dagmar, never found anyone at all.

She was too old now to find young love like Mercy, and Florence definitely didn't want to end up alone like Aunt Dagmar, who had an austere and slightly unpleasant demeanor. She'd come to visit once and found fault with everything and everyone of her sisters. When she left, her stepmother had told her that Aunt Dagmar was bitter because she had never married.

Florence looked over at her stepmother, who was now nodding off with the needle in her hand. "Careful you don't stick yourself with the needle."

Wilma opened her eyes and blinked rapidly.

"Perhaps it's time for bed," Florence suggested.

"Already?" Wilma looked over at her. "It's nice to sit here without constant chatter and I was enjoying your company."

Florence was pleased to hear it. "All right. I'll stay up a little longer if you can stay awake. I can't stop thinking how well-suited Stephen and Mercy are."

"*Jah. Gott* has blessed us and them."

"He has. *Mamm,* why were you so set on finding a man for Mercy?"

"Because getting married was all she could talk about, and she's the oldest."

"She's not, though. I am."

"Florence, that has nothing to do with it. She's the oldest born to me, but you are every bit my *dochder.* I didn't think you were interested."

"I am interested." It was nice to hear those words from *Mamm's* mouth. Wilma was the only mother she remembered other than a couple of very hazy and happy memories of her birth-mother. *Dat* and other people had told her she resembled her mother, but she had no way of knowing because photographs were never taken among the Amish.

"I always thought you would stay on here and help with the orchard. This is the income for us all. It was a harsh blow to us all when Mark left, and then Earl too."

"Maybe, just maybe, I'll want to marry one day."

"Yeah, and you should." Her stepmother opened her mouth to say something else, but no words came out. Then she closed her lips.

"Don't worry about it."

"Do you want me to help you find a husband like I helped Mercy?"

Florence chuckled. *"Nee.* I can find my own. Not that I'm going to look. It'll happen if it's meant to."

"Of course it will. I thought you might've met someone at your half *schweschder's* wedding."

"I didn't." Florence had hoped to meet someone at every wedding she'd gone to from the time she'd been a teenager.

"I hoped having the wedding here might've encouraged Stephen to stay in our community. What did you think?"

"There's no use talking about that now. She's gone for a year, but they both said they'd be back. Stephen was a tremendous help to us in the orchard." They could certainly use Stephen's help on his return and not just at harvest time.

"It would've been nice if your *vadder* had been here for the wedding. I miss him."

"Me too." Florence couldn't look at Wilma because she knew they'd both cry. She missed her father unbelievably. After her mother died, it had been just the four of them—her and her two older brothers and *Dat*, but not for long.

She was just a small girl when *Dat* married Wilma. Earl had come for Mercy's wedding, but hadn't even stayed with them and she'd barely gotten to talk with him. Ever since Mark married Christina, they hardly saw either of them. Seeing Mark meant she had to see Christina and that was often a chore.

Several minutes later, Florence looked over at Wilma and saw her eyes closed and her mouth wide open. She giggled to herself. As she decided to call it a night, she wrapped up her crochet project and put it on the small side table next to the couch. Then she very carefully lifted the cross stitch fabric from her stepmother's lap, inserted the needle, and laid it on the table, too.

"Gut nacht," Florence whispered to her sleeping stepmother before she headed upstairs for bed. She unbraided her thigh-length hair and pulled her brush through it thinking about her half-sisters. Honor wanted to marry Jonathon, that was no secret, but it was troubling how Cherish was already interested in love at such a young age. If one of her *bruders* were still at home, she might not have had to be so strict. She placed her brush back onto her chest of drawers.

As she slipped between the cool sheets, she wondered if she'd ever marry.

She turned off the gas lamp on her nightstand, and then buried her head in her pillow, thinking about Carter Braithwaite. He'd never suit her, but she was certain God was using him as a sign. A sign that there was a good Amish man out there for her somewhere. If Mercy had found a man so suddenly, one who was so perfectly suited, there was definite hope for her.

"Bonnet sisters—humph," she murmured as she pulled her quilt higher around her shoulders.

Thank you for reading Amish Mercy.

www.SamanthaPriceAuthor.com

THE NEXT BOOK IN THE SERIES

Book 2 Amish Honor

At just seventeen, Honor Baker found herself an unlikely love—her new brother-in-law. When the couple learns they won't be allowed to marry, their choice is obvious, and they do the only thing that makes sense. When Honor goes missing, Florence finds herself in a car on a road trip with her mysterious *Englisher* neighbor.

A NOTE FROM SAMANTHA

I'm often asked how my stories come about and how I come up with the ideas, so I'll share my inspiration for The Amish Bonnet Sisters series.

I grew up listening to my mother's memories of her childhood. Her favorite ones were of staying at the family's dairy farm. She was often sent there for her aunts to look after when she was a young girl.

A few years ago, my mother started telling me about her Aunt Florence.

Florence was the oldest of thirteen girls (no boys), and she did everything for the family. They lived on a large dairy farm and had a reasonably tough life. While Florence's mother was busy having babies, Florence ran the household, looked after her younger sisters, and worked, milking the cows by hand alongside her father. I was amazed by Florence being the backbone of the family at such a young age. She was the real-life Florence that inspired Florence Baker of the Amish Bonnet Sisters.

I do hope you will enjoy spending time at the Baker Apple Orchard as much as I have.

Much love & blessings.

Samantha Price
www.SamanthaPriceAuthor.com

ALL SAMANTHA PRICE'S BOOK SERIES

Amish Maids Trilogy
A 3 book Amish romance series of novels featuring 5 friends finding love.

Amish Love Blooms
A 6 book Amish romance series of novels about four sisters and their cousins.

Amish Misfits
A series of 7 stand-alone books about people who have never fitted in.

The Amish Bonnet Sisters
To date there are 28 books in this continuing family saga. My most popular and best-selling series.

Amish Women of Pleasant Valley
An 8 book Amish romance series with the same characters. This has been one of my most popular series.

Ettie Smith Amish Mysteries
An ongoing cozy mystery series with octogenarian sleuths. Popular with lovers of mysteries such as Miss Marple or Murder She Wrote.

Amish Secret Widows' Society
A ten novella mystery/romance series - a prequel to the Ettie Smith Amish Mysteries.

Expectant Amish Widows

A stand-alone Amish romance series of 19 books.

Seven Amish Bachelors
A 7 book Amish Romance series following the Fuller brothers' journey to finding love.

Amish Foster Girls
A 4 book Amish romance series with the same characters who have been fostered to an Amish family.

Amish Brides
An Amish historical romance. 5 book series with the same characters who have arrived in America to start their new life.

Amish Romance Secrets
The first series I ever wrote. 6 novellas following the same characters.

Amish Christmas Books

Each year I write an Amish Christmas stand-alone romance novel.

Amish Twin Hearts
A 4 book Amish Romance featuring twins and their friends.

Amish Wedding Season
The second series I wrote. It has the same characters throughout the 5 books.

Amish Baby Collection
Sweet Amish Romance series of 6 stand-alone novellas.

Gretel Koch Jewel Thief
A clean 5 book suspense/mystery series about a jewel thief who has agreed to consult with the FBI.

Made in the USA
Columbia, SC
09 December 2023